The BOOK *of* WORDS

The BOOK of WORDS

JENNY ERPENBECK

****

Translated, with an Afterword, by

SUSAN BERNOFSKY

A NEW DIRECTIONS BOOK

Originally published in Germany under the title *Wörterbuch* by Eichborn Verlag.

Manufactured in the United States of America
First published as a New Directions Paperbook (1092) in 2007.

Library of Congress Cataloging-in-Publication Data

Erpenbeck, Jenny, 1967–
    [Wörterbuch. English]
    The Book of Words / Jenny Erpenbeck ;
    translated, with an afterword, by Susan Bernofsky.
       p. cm.
    ISBN-13: 978-0-8112-1706-4 (alk. paper)
    I. Bernofsky, Susan. II. Title.
    PT2665.R59W6713 2007
    401'.4—dc22

                       2007023569

9 8 7 6

NEW DIRECTIONS BOOKS ARE PUBLISHED FOR JAMES LAUGHLIN
BY NEW DIRECTIONS PUBLISHING CORPORATION
80 EIGHTH AVENUE, NEW YORK, NY 10011

The Book of Words

11

****

Translator's Afterword

91

For my father, with all my heart

"Usually all that's left is a few bones."
— SCHIMMECK

"An entire generation disappeared here."
— FONDERBRIDER

... *bên zi bêna, bluot zi bluoda*
lid zi geliden, sôse gelîmida sîn!

... bone to bone, blood to blood
limb to limbs, thus be they bonded.
— 2ND MERSEBURG INCANTATION

WHAT ARE MY EYES for if they can see but see nothing? What are my ears for if they can hear but hear nothing? Why all this strangeness inside my head?

All of it must be thought into nothingness, one whorl of gray matter at a time, until in the end a spoonful of me will be left glistening at the bottom. I must seize memory like a knife and turn it against itself, stabbing memory with memory. If I can.

Father and mother. Ball. Car. These might be the only words that were still intact when I learned them. Then even they got turned around, ripped out of me and stuck back in upside-down, making the opposite of ball ball, the opposite of father and mother father and mother. What is a car? All the other words had silent halves dragging them down from the start like lead weights around ankles, just as the moon lugs its dark half around with it even when it's full. But it keeps circling in its orbit all the same. For me, words used to be stable, fixed in place, but now I'm letting them all go, if need be I'll cut off a foot if that's the only way to get rid of them. Ball. Ball.

Lullaby and goodnight. My mother is putting me to bed. She strokes my head as she sings. White, dry hand stroking the head of a child. *With roses bedight.* Eyes the color of water gazing at me; already my eyelids are falling shut. *With lilies o'erspread,* she sings. But lilies are for funerals. Not these lilies, she'd say if she saw the words were making me cry again, they aren't real lilies at all, they're just lilies-of-the-valley for faeries to sleep under. But tonight it's already too late for crying, I've traveled too far into the land of sleep to turn around, and they aren't lilies-of-the-valley, they're real lilies that someone I don't know is going to lay on my coffin and nail it shut as I sleep. *Lay thee down now and rest,* she sings. She pulls the blanket up to my chin and turns out the light. The coffin nails scrape my skin, lots of little bloody wounds. *May thy slumbers be blessed.* And what if they aren't blessed? Then I'll remain lying here in my coffin-bed forever. *May thy slumbers be blessed.* And the drops of blood will turn to stone. Mother.

A ball is a thing that rolls and sometimes bounces. A father is a man who stays taller than you for a long time. Before my father goes to confession, he shaves and puts on a clean shirt. If a person wanted to play ball with someone's head, only the nose would get in the way. Before my father goes to confession, he takes me on his lap and lets me ride his knees. Many, many children have already ridden into this landscape and become fodder for ravens, countless white-skinned screeching riders who never seem to manage a full gallop before they've tumbled down into the bog between their fathers' knees. My father's shirt smells fresh and is rough when I bury my head in it after I've pulled myself up out of the bog with a motion that makes me dizzy every time. Father.

House. Our house is the exact center of the garden. Pink walls, the pink bleached by the sun and already flaking. I slip a fingernail beneath the plaster and snap it off. Underneath, an ocher color comes to light. When I tap a rock against this hidden paint, yet another layer of skin appears in the islands that result: gray. I can't go any deeper than this, the gray clings firmly to the walls of the house, perhaps this gray really is the house itself. My mother says: Stop that. I know, I know: If I want to go into the house, I can use the front door.

From sunshine to shade. Naked soles padding from the dust outside to the cool stone. Barefoot. The sun is almost always shining here, it shines and shines and shines, and the sky around the sun is almost always completely empty. What does the sun eat? I ask my father. Water, he replies. And where is its bed? The sun doesn't sleep, he says. When it is nighttime here, he says, the sun is shining on the other side of the world. Lovely weather today. Today and every day.

Why didn't you have any milk for me, I ask my mother. Some women have a lot of milk, and others none at all, my mother replies. I can remember my wet nurse's breasts quite clearly. I drank from them for a long time. Longer than any other child I know, my mother says. Even after I started school, the first thing I would do when I came home was sit down on my nurse's lap and drink. Her milk was watery and sweet, her breasts rosy and full, firm islands on the body of an aging woman. My wet nurse—who even after I had stopped drinking from her held my entire child-hood in her lap like an apple—resembled a faerie with green, slanting eyes, one who had been cast out of a faerie tale and now appeared rather somber, thanks to her hair, which had grown darker at the roots and then turned gray, and the colors she wore even in the hottest summer, autumnal hues: brown, black and olive green. To what I saw, I added an invisible, pointed, cone-shaped hat, light blue with a veil. That's just not normal, my mother had said once as she watched me drink from the faerie breasts, and she'd tried to dismiss my wet nurse. For three entire days I refused to speak, and on the fourth the nurse returned. Milk. Drink.

I never saw my wet nurse's garden. I don't know whether the shoebox with the hands fell on the grass or into a flowerbed. It doesn't matter, my wet nurse says to me when I drop my ice cream; she buys me another one. Where my fallen ice cream is melting in the sun, it leaves a bright splotch on the asphalt. Marie, my wet nurse's daughter, has much longer fingers than I do and never drops her ice cream. And her hands are always clean, no matter what dirty things she touches. My hands are always exactly as sticky and dusty as the things we play with and eat, or as the city streets we fall down on when we're running or push and shove one another. As if her skin were different, though when I take Marie's hand—Marie who is in a matter of speaking my milk-sister—her skin feels just like mine. As if it were actually made of wax or stone so the dirt slides right off. *Our Father, who art in Heaven.* At night when I am lying alone in bed, I creep all the way under the covers and fold my hands, which I have rubbed clean with an eraser to make them just like Marie's; by praying, I am now drawing all of Heaven down into the dark with me, including Our Father. Say good morning, shake hands, shake hands.

Those who, and then their friends, then the ones who remember them, then all who are afraid, and finally everyone. My father says these words behind a closed door in our house, at the time the door still looks huge to me, I imagine what would happen if it were to fall on me while I am pressed against it, listening, wonder whether I'd be crushed flat, through the door the smell of tobacco is filtering into the hall—everyone—and whether it would make a noise when it fell on me, or whether a door like that falls quietly upon a body made of flesh. The next day, hopping from island to island across the city's stone carpet patterns, holding my mother's hand, I count off silently: Those who. Then their friends. The ones who remember. Who are afraid. And finally everyone. Either always the black stones or always the white ones or always the gray, holding my mother's hand. This sentence is like a counting-out rhyme, and like a counting-out rhyme it cannot stop until it reaches the end—I can't interrupt my hopping in the middle, can't just freeze on one leg somewhere in the city, standing on black or white or gray. I am afraid for my father. Everyone. Everyone everyone.

A bird was walking here, my father says. Squatting down beside me, he points out the star-shaped scratches in the dark soil at the edge of our garden, in the shade of the trees where no grass grows. *There were three ravens sat on a tree.* What is a track, I ask my father. A trace that is left behind, something that cannot be caused by chance, my father replies. *They were as black as black might be.* But then before you can know what cannot be caused by chance, I say, you have to know everything else. Probably, my father says. And what about the double time a track like this has. What double time, my father says. The time, I say, when the bird was walking here, and then the second time, when we see it was here—the track is a sort of bridge between them. Perhaps, my father says. But by the time you're finally old enough to tell the difference between chance and everything else, you're too heavy to walk across the bridge. No, my father says, that's silly, and he picks up a little stick and starts making star-shaped scratches beside the star-shaped scratches.

Day after day, my father works in a palace whose exterior is perfectly white. In this palace my father sees to it that things are orderly. Wailing sirens, flashing lights. White walls, white columns, white front steps, blinding sun gleaming off the building as if the building itself were the sun, only the trees to the right and left of it are dark, and there is never a wind stirring their leaves. Wailing, flashing. I wonder whether the windows are just painted on, since the palace always stands there so quietly, my mother says everything inside it is orderly and well looked after, my father keeps everything in order, and I never see anyone at the windows. It might well be that the building's been walled up, that's why its exterior gleams like that, sunlight cannot enter and get lost inside. Flashing lights. Just as my mother looks after me. Do you comb order, do you give order something to eat and drink? In a building which no light ever enters, in which you have to hold on to the walls and feel your way about because all the windows have been bricked up. More wailing. If you can't find order in the dark, might you accidentally comb the air instead of it, or upset the food and drink, and does order remain there all the same: dirty, un-combed, ravenous and running wild? Wails upon wails, an explosion of lights. My father comes out of the building, thank goodness, he's holding one hand to his eyes because at first the sun blinds him, but then he sees us, my mother and me, standing at the foot of the steps, it's Friday at half past two, we're picking him up from work as we do every Friday, he runs quickly down the steps and kisses me with his lips that are as soft as a woman's. My father never wears a uniform, and the cars lined up before the building are gray and white, no flashing lights anywhere. Where have the sirens gone wailing off to? They turned into birds, my wet nurse says. It is sunny and quiet in the middle of our city where the police live.

A miracle, my mother says and points at two black-clad, billowing angels who, hand in hand far off in the distance, are plummeting from the sky above the ocean, the sky is blue, utterly blue, just as blue as the water in which it is mirrored, the angels are plunging from blue to blue, from sky to water, plunging black against the blue with their arms spread wide, holding one another's hands, my mother and I are standing down below at the harbor observing this miracle, and many other people are standing there as well, pointing at the angels and crossing themselves.

Red, green and yellow, us on the ground. Orange. The wind slips beneath the angels' clothes, white, white wind, only the clothing of these angels is black, why black, I ask my mother. Black. Black isn't a color.

Or does black come about because you've thrown all the colors together in a single pot. I am sitting on the living room rug, cutting animals I like out of magazines while my mother is off in the kitchen washing lettuce, stirring and chopping, and my father is squatting beside me on the rug holding the paper taut and saying things like: Careful, watch the ears. It's always evening when my father sits beside me on the rug, sometimes even nighttime. When I look up at his head, which I have to look up to see even when he's squatting beside me, that's how tall he is, it appears framed, evening after evening, in the dark rectangle of the un-curtained window behind him. Shiny smooth blackness, no moon-light, and before it this head belonging to my father, which appears light by contrast: blond, light-brown eyes, and teeth like pearls when he opens his mouth and says what is in the pictures. Is it true that a vulture can seize an entire live lamb and carry it up to the sky and then drop it somewhere to eat it? Of course not, my father says, a vulture only eats things that are already dead. He strokes my head while I am cutting out the little lamb. Dinner's ready, my mother calls, we get up and suddenly the entire living room is reflected in that same window and the blackness vanishes. But behind the reflection it is still there, this impenetrable black-ness, I know this because the garden, which lies on the other side of the window, is hidden from view all night long. The window has captured the garden and won't let it out, it's thrown a black cloth over it and now is trying to trick us with the colorful reflec-tion of our living room.

In the morning the garden has returned to view, I could prob-ably even walk around in it if I didn't have to go to school; trees and flowers have been released from captivity, someone has pulled off the black cloth, folded it up and hidden it away somewhere, but only temporarily, until night falls once more, this much is certain. Morning after morning the skirt, knee-highs and shoes in blue, and the shirt with short or long sleeves, white. Just like the others. For years on end, morning after morning: the blue cap on my head, a folded ship made of felt, upside-down as if capsized and fixed in place with a bobby pin, a gold insignia on one side. In the grass the dew glistens, my feet would get cold and damp now if I went outside barefoot, instead I slip into my shoes and lay the scarf, the same blue as the cap, around my neck and tie the knot, a knot that makes the knot itself invisible, my father taught it to me years ago, even before I started school. Blue the sky was, utterly and perfectly blue. Now I look exactly like the others in all the places where my body is covered with fabric.

Present colors! This command, issued to the honor guard by a girl standing in front of the assembly, calls our eyes to order. Now all of us are required to gaze at the three pupils who are bringing us the flag, the one marching in front is the flag-bearer, he holds the pole to which the flag is affixed, and the two others walking behind him form the honor guard's train, the flag itself has no train and hangs straight down because no wind is blowing. All eyes are fixed on the trio with the flag, we stand in the schoolyard in a square, only one edge of this square has been left open, the one facing the entrance to the school, and it is to the center of this open edge that the honor guard is marching, the rest of us stand along the other three sides of the square with the smallest in front and the taller ones in back, each row of toes lining up perfectly, right hands held to caps in a salute, and from this moment on I can no longer allow my gaze to wander across the blue and white water above which the other children's heads are bobbing like flesh-colored buoys, heads that cannot be made identical to one another without masks, no more than can the naked bits of knee sticking out between stockings and skirts, knees that are crooked, fat or pointy, scraped or dimpled, but definitely tan in this land of eternal summer. I gaze at the flag and wonder whether the teachers who have stipulated where our eyes must rest can see our gazes crisscrossing through the air, aimed at the trio with the flag like so many lances.

One. Two. And three. During the first three years of school, we are required to cross our arms if we wish to rest them on our desktops when we aren't writing. Only when we are older, the teachers say, will we be permitted to lay one arm smooth and straight atop the other. When we pray, each hand rests flat against the other, no interlocking of fingers allowed. When it's time for recess, we exit the classroom one behind the other in single file, nice and slow, the teachers say. One. Two. And three. All rapid motions, everything that is sudden or askew, all running, swinging, shoving, lolling and falling, all spinning in circles and jumping has been cut off from us, brought to a place where it is inaccessible to us and left for scrap. Just like bicycles no longer fit for use, all these things twist together in a heap, intertwining to form a mass that can never again be disentangled, and in the end all of it decomposes collectively, as if it had always been of a piece. One.

During recess we crouch in the shade of the big tree—no shouting, children, no fighting—gathering up the firebugs that live at the base of its trunk, filling our hands with them, or else with gravel and grains of sand, and when an airplane flies past overhead, one of us whispers louder than the other: My parents are up there, they're on their way to Alaska, or: That's my mother's airplane, she's traveling to Rome, or: Today my father's sitting in that plane up there, he's flying far far away, where's he going, really far away, well if you don't even know where he's going then it can't be true, yes it is, my father's even flying across the ocean, well so where's he going. Really far away. That's stupid. No shouting.

We're winning, my friend Anna whispers to us, we're winning, she always says when a tire blows out somewhere outside, the noise it makes sounds like gunfire, sometimes there are many shots in a row. We're winning, she whispers, and then all of us fall silent, waiting to see if we really are winning.

This time we didn't win, my friend Anna says a day later. My mother, she says, climbed over the fence to give the horses something to eat. And one of the horses wasn't really tame yet, it shied away from her and didn't want to eat anything. And when she got closer, it reared up on its hind legs. And then, I ask. Then it came down on its hooves and almost hit my mother in the head, so she tried to run away. But she didn't manage to get back over the fence in time, and then the horse saw she was scared of it and came after her. And if she hadn't been afraid? Then the horse would have remained calm. But it saw she was afraid. And then it came after her and kicked her and threw itself on top of her with all its weight. But horses never kick people, I say. Not if they're tame, Anna says, but this horse was basically still wild. Oh, I say. And then the other horses got carried away as well. They remembered how they used to be wild. And then? Then all the horses ran over my mother. With their hooves. My mother was an Indian, Anna says to me. I don't say anything. She climbed over the fence to feed her horses, she says, and then her very own horses trampled her to death. Just imagine, Anna says to me. I imagine this, and then say to my friend: I think that's a good way for an Indian to die. I think so too, Anna says. Were you there? I ask. No, Anna says. And the horses? They had to shoot them, of course. You heard the shots yourself. Yes, I say, that's true.

A music box is playing: *Plume in the summer wind, waywardly swaying, thus heart of womankind everyway bendeth*. The music box is on a table with wheels that my mother and father roll into my room in the morning. Flowers and candlelight, and beside the music box are the presents. It's my birthday. One day out of all the days of the year is the day when I was born. One day out of all the days of the year is the first day. Or is it better just to dive into the wet concrete right away and let the first day be the last. Open your eyes, behold the grave and then dive right in and turn to stone. *Plume in the summer wind.* I am given a silver barrette, a book of faerie tales, letter paper with a watermark and my name in the upper left-hand corner, a soup dish on the bottom of which two girls are playing ball, and a Rose of Jericho, a dried-up thing that becomes a flower when you wet it. Until the dish breaks, the girls will go on playing ball at the bottom of the porcelain. Until water is in sight, the Rose of Jericho will keep rolling through the desert. The dish will not break. When I have spooned up enough soup that the girls begin to play beneath the noodles and greens, I put my ear to the dish to listen, I want to hear one or the other of them catching the ball. My mother says there's nothing to hear because the ball is suspended in midair between them. And it will never come down? No, my mother says, it's a picture. We are so happy you were born. A picture always remains just as it is.

Saint Difunta Correa died of thirst in the desert, but the child drinking at her breast was still alive when the two of them were found. Drinking life from a dead woman, my wet nurse smoothes the little picture with her index finger, it's odd, when the life leaves a body, this makes it heavier rather than lighter. The saint's back, legs and heels press heavily into the sand as she holds the child in her arms, yes, holds it, the dead woman is still holding a living child in her arms, which are already dead, and the third figure in this alliance is the silent sun beating down upon the two of them, the sun that caused the death of the mother. Wherever there is an altar in the sand for this saint who died of thirst, travelers leave bottles of water as offerings, my wet nurse says. I wonder whether the water can summon her back to life. Whether a saint who has been dead so long can drink her life back out of all these many sealed bottles. Does a saint even have hands and a mouth. My wet nurse says she will most assuredly get up again. Yes, but when. When no one comes any longer to leave new offerings, she says. When silence reigns on earth, she won't be able to resist looking to see what's going on, then at the latest she will get up again and drink.

So the story does go on. To the right and left and above and below the edges of the picture. Of course, my wet nurse says. And only as far as the picture extends do things remain as they are. That's right, she says, and lets me hold the little card with the image of the Difunta. But all around the picture things remain in motion, I ask, even this story itself which cannot go any farther here in the picture. Most certainly, my wet nurse says. You can see, she says, how for example the sun is moving across the sky. Yes, I say, that's true, that's how you can tell. It would be awful, she says, if the sun were always as high up in the sky as here above the two people in the picture. It would burn everything up. That's true, I say, looking at the bars of light on the floor of my room put there by the sun slipping between the blinds. My wet nurse takes back the picture of the saint and puts it in her olive-colored bag. Outside it's noon.

I wonder if the sun can wear out. In countries like this, where it must shine day after day all year round, does it get shabby more quickly than elsewhere. In countries like this, where it can see everything at almost every moment except during the night or when, as rarely happens, it is raining, is the sun marked by what it sees. Are the things taking place beneath its rays reflected back at it. So that the sun itself, depending what it illuminates, appears perfect or rumpled, healthy or cold. Is this what sometimes makes it turn white. Or blotchy. All that looking. Probably. While I kneel and get up again and sit down again and then kneel again, per-forming the roundelay of prayer Sunday after Sunday in the crepuscular church, I am thinking of the Holy Trinity: mother, infant and sun.

Hot, my mother says, pulling me away from the stove. Hot, my father says whenever anyone's making a fire, and he positions himself between me and the fire. Hot, my mother says as she lights the candle to place inside my St. Martin's Day lantern. *Star light star bright, first star I see tonight.* When the candle's little shade has been drawn all around it like an accordion, I am permitted to take the lantern by its long wooden stick and go outside with it. *I wish I may, I wish I might.* The shade is made of paper. Am I made of paper too, I ask my mother. My mother laughs and says: Of course not, and calls out to my father that I just asked if I was made of paper, and my father laughs too, comes out of his room into the hallway and fondles my head. Then I go out onto the street with my mother and see children coming out of all the other houses with lanterns in their hands, on St. Martin's we're all allowed to stay up past midnight and brighten the dark streets with our lanterns. If I were made of paper, first my dress would catch fire, then my legs, then my arms, then my head, basically all the parts farthest from the center, and only then would my stomach start to burn, and the little pink buttons above my heart, and finally the heart itself, the most interior part of me. All these things would turn black and keep flying up into the night as long as they continued to smolder, and only after the air had cooled them down would they return to earth in a rain of ashes. But I am not made of paper, my mother repeats. Nonetheless she pulls me away any time I want to touch fire, saying: Hot.

Eyes, nose, mouth. How often my mother shut her eyes the instant before my index finger hit its mark, how often my father opened his mouth to show me what a mouth is and then closed it around my finger as if he were going to bite, but he didn't bite. If you wanted to play ball with someone's head, only one thing would get in the way: the nose. My father's teeth are very white, and when I probe around inside his dark mouth with my finger, they feel damp and hard. I see a tree and say tree, I smell the cake my mother bakes on Sunday and say cake, I hear a bird twittering in the garden, and my mother says: That's right, a bird. We put the cake into our mouths, it vanishes there, mouth, eyes and nose: holes, the beginnings of paths, no one knows quite where they lead. Stomach, my mother says, I've never seen my stomach from the inside, but at least what I eat comes out again on the other end, and what about the things I put into my eyes, where do they go, are all of them supposed to fit inside my head, even if I were to stack them up the way our housekeeper stacks the laundry, folding it and placing one piece atop the other, there still wouldn't be room, I don't think, and therefore I keep saying all the things I'm seeing so they'll change course inside my head and go out again through my mouth. Shit, I say later when I see what has become of the cake. That's a filthy word, my mother says, wiping my bottom. Don't say words like that, she says and flushes. But it's something we ate. That was before, my mother says, and we go back to the other room. So the cake has gotten dirty on its way through my body. You can't look at it that way, my father says, it doesn't have anything to do with you, it's just a matter of the word. I'm not allowed to say it. No, my mother says, words like that should never cross the lips of a young lady. Eyes. Nose. Mouth. So it's precisely the things that are filthy that are supposed to be stacked up and stored in my head and aren't allowed to change course and go out again through my mouth. But, I say, if I see a foot that is dirty and say foot, then that's a filthy word too, isn't it, but my mother says no, the word itself is clean. Aha. It's only the word shit I'm not supposed to say, but now that's really quite enough, my mother says. My father says: time for a walk. The obelisk stands at the eye of the city, on the large square with cars circling around it, since yesterday it's been wearing a wooden skirt; I slide my hand across the white letters on the fence boards, there's a spotlight shining on them, and my father reads aloud: Silence is health.

Maintaining an equilibrium, my father said one day when I came home from school with my hair disheveled, by no means depends on the physical strength possessed by you or your opponent, equilibrium is always an equilibrium of the means you employ. On this occasion my father showed me a maneuver that lets you twist an attacking arm onto your opponent's back before he even knows what's happening and in this way hold and overpower him. Whenever I played shop as a little girl, I always gave my customers play money along with the marbles I was selling instead of requesting payment. I hadn't yet understood that even in buying and selling there is an invisible equilibrium to be upheld, one utterly indifferent to the often shabby appearance of the coins. If all the maneuvers my father has employed while rubbing the holster of his service weapon until it is shiny have served to preserve some equilibrium or other, then this light, invisible weapon assuredly balances out many things whose nature is not immediately apparent to me upon gazing only at his gun or its holster.

But this time we won, my friend Anna says to me in the schoolyard, nudging the ball this way and that with her feet. No one in the whole world plays better than we do. We're the champions. Anna's soccer ball hits a pebble and changes course. Two to one, she says, now it's been proven. She runs after the ball. And that's why they're setting off fireworks now, she shouts, coming to a halt beside the ball, we can hear the explosions, but because the brick wall all around our schoolyard is so high and perhaps also because, as always, the sun is shining, we can see neither flowers nor rings of fire nor shooting stars nor golden rain in the sky. Maybe they forgot about the sun, Anna says, stepping back at an angle for a running start, then she kicks the ball, shooting it at me, that is, at the goal behind me, which I am guarding, I'm the goalie, and the goal is a bit of grass between an empty milk carton on the right and a stone wastepaper basket on the left, I step to one side of the goal I am guarding, and the ball hurtles into it. If it had struck me, I'd be dead. That isn't fair, Anna says. Plenty of room on a soccer field like this, and as for the grass, the softer the better. Body after body beneath the grass, hands outspread, and above all these hands, mouths and eyes, the ball rolls toward the goal and gently glides into it, we're the champions.

I am sleeping. My grandmother is telling my aunt how she got dizzy that morning. A free-of-charge carousel ride, she says, all the cupboards were dancing around me in a circle, I was seeing stars, and then everything went black. Then I heard the angels singing, my grandmother says. Free of charge. She laughs. My mother says to her brother, my uncle: All the same, I think it's funny she hasn't called. After all, she's our sister. I even told her she could stay with us. And my aunt laughs too and says, oh, you don't even have to be so old to fall, our neighbor fell off the roof of his shed last Sunday, he wanted to look over the edge to see if he'd left his hammer down there, so he bent over, but then his rear end wanted to look too and came sliding down on top of him, and the next thing he knew he was lying on the ground. The neighbor. Well, maybe he'd also had a bit too much to drink, my grandmother says. Quite possible, my aunt replies. My uncle says, you've got to remember what she must be going through with such a husband. Well, then let her bring him too, my mother says. My uncle doesn't say anything. None of this makes any sense to me, my mother says. My uncle says to my father, two to one, not bad, eh? And my father replies, we're the champions now. My uncle says, I never thought I'd see the day, and laughs, and my father laughs too, and my aunt says, well, it's true a person shouldn't start drinking in the morning, and my grandmother gives no response. I am lying on the floor, asleep. My mother says, how can she sleep like that, on the floor in the middle of the room, and everyone looks at me for a moment, no one says anything, then my mother says, let me go see if dinner's ready. My aunt says, but you definitely shouldn't wash the windows by yourself anymore, that ladder really is dangerous. My mother calls out: Dinner's ready. *Be present at our table, Lord, be here and everywhere adored. Your mercies bless, and grant that we may feast in Paradise with Thee.*

The table we sit down at is large and oval, like a stadium. Uncle and aunt, mother and father, father at the narrow curve at the end of the table, grandmother beside me. There's fish for dinner. The young woman at the far end of the table, directly opposite my father, declines without a word when the housekeeper wants to put some on her plate. The young man sitting to my left also helps himself only to vegetables. The housekeeper plucks a thread from his shirt before she goes on serving, and my mother says: The flies are such a nuisance this year. The housekeeper smiles at me. The two strangers slowly manipulate their knives and forks, silently chewing. I point at them with my knife, asking who these people are who are eating with us, but before my question can slip out between fish and bones, my grandmother says, don't wave your knife around in the air, and my mother says, don't talk when you're eating fish.

Snow. Knives and forks clinking against porcelain, jawbones hinging open with a faint cracking sound, my father pulverizes the fish-bones between his teeth instead of drawing them out of his mouth one by one, the sparkling water sings in its goblets. If snow were to start falling now, falling on the tablecloth, on the hair of my mother and father, on hands and into goblets, then eventually you wouldn't hear any of this any longer. In the beginning, the snow will melt because the things it is falling on are still warm, that's what my grandmother told me, but sooner or later the cold starts to get the better of the warmth, she said, that's always how it goes if it keeps snowing long enough, the snow covers every-thing up and then all is still. If it were to start snowing now, the entire family would fall silent all at once. White, soft and as mo-tionless as the fish we are eating. My grandmother is the only one in our family who can still remember snow.

When my grandmother was a young girl, she once laced her legs so tightly into ice skates that to this day you can see purple marks under her knees. Snow is edible, she said. She sewed a lit-tle cap for my mother during that one cold winter she spent with her in the old country, a cap that could be tied beneath the chin, with a wooly ball on top. So my mother too was once an infant, but far from here, long ago, on the other side of the world, wrapped up in blankets, lying on a sled with frozen-red cheeks—which in this black-and-white photograph are distinctly gray. On the other side of the world. The surface of the photo has cracks in it because of the long journey on which my grandmother carried it with her. But to this day the cap remains undamaged, it lies in a stack of carnival costumes in a heavy leather suitcase in the store-room. My mother's eyes are the color of water, they look like melted snow. My eyes are black. I don't know what snow is, and there was never a time when I did know this. On this side of the world.

When fish is served, everyone is given a special knife that isn't sharp. But when we are eating meat, I have to use my child's knife, the handle of which has a cat's face engraved in it. Then my mother cuts my meat into little pieces with her knife, which is pointed and jagged-edged, and my knife with the cat is only for pushing the bits she's cut onto my fork. The handle of my fork has a bear on it, and the spoon has a rabbit. If a knife is sharp enough, you can cut all the way around the soles of a man's or even a woman's feet and then peel back the skin. After all, this man or this woman will no longer have far to walk to reach the land of the dead. And some word is always the last one. Knife perhaps. Or some other one. Some word this man or this woman has always known.

No one knows for sure anymore, my wet nurse says to me, whether the Difunta had already given birth to her child before she set out on her journey or whether the child was born in the desert. Why did she take a trip in the first place, I ask. The child's father was imprisoned one hundred and fifty kilometers away, she replies. Behind bars on the other side of the desert. She was on her way to see him, my wet nurse says.

Did you know, Marie says, that where our garden is there used to be desert. Marie is scooping sand into a small metal pail with her hands. I have never seen the garden belonging to my wet nurse and her daughter Marie, who is something like my milk-sister. A long time before I was born, Marie says, my mother stuck a few scrawny little trees into the desert and hoped for rain. And did it rain, I ask. Uh-huh, says Marie, whose bucket is nearly full already. Next to the bucket I have been digging a hole with a shovel and finally have reached the depth at which the sand becomes firmer and shimmers dark and moist at the edges of the pit. The shadows the trees cast on the sand are no thicker than threads of tar, but in these threads the rain has gotten caught. Now I can finally empty the sugar sand from Marie's bucket into my hole. Later everything grew. Flowers. Even grass. That's right, Marie says, and gets up so as to take me by one hand and one foot and spin me around in a circle so fast that my own weight carries me out of this orbit into the sand. I land right in a thicket of unfamiliar arms and legs.

My wet nurse is sitting in the shade beneath an umbrella, her skin very white against the brown pattern of her bathing suit. This section of beach is reserved for women and children, and beside it is the section for men. Swimming lovers tryst along the rope that cuts the sea in two, touching beneath the water's surface. In places where warm and cold water are not clearly separated, my father told me not long ago, currents are produced, the intersection of the warm and the cold sets the water in motion. My father knows all about currents. From time to time, little groups of women rise to their feet on the beach and start clapping their hands, one of them holding on her shoulder the child that has lost track of its mother, nanny or aunt and now is crying. Mother, nanny or aunt hears the clapping and comes running up to claim her child. Gray-haired old women are playing cards, the heads of women are lying there, eyes closed, and feet running down to the water thrust their toes into the sand between the cheeks of these women, children are building sand castles and moats that fill up and empty again with each wave. There is plenty of empty space between the men on the other side, but here where the women and children are, each lying, sitting or standing body is packed in among many others.

When I get home from the beach, sand between my toes, my hair matted from the salt water, I find the young woman who ate with us not long ago sitting in my room on the sofa, reading a book. Her clothes are covered with dust. I was just passing the time until you came back, she says, and lays the book aside. Could I have something to drink. I say: One moment, and go down to the kitchen. I open the icebox and gaze into it for a while: sausage, cheese, yogurt. I gaze into it. Fruit, vegetables, ketchup and eggs. I shiver. A pot filled with yesterday's leftovers. I gaze into the cool, illuminated window, and everything I might be capable of thinking freezes solid. There is a half-full bottle of mineral water in the icebox door, I grab it and a glass and bring both of them to where my visitor is waiting. Do you know how to swim, the woman asks me after she has filled the glass with water and emptied it in a single draught. Yes, I say. When I was your age, she says, I used to dive for combs. In the ocean, I ask. No, in the swimming pool, of course, she says, smiling. The sea, she says, carries off everything you throw in it, quicker than you can imagine. My father knows all about currents, I say. I see, the woman says.

She's got a fever, my father says, laying his heavy hand on my forehead. I am lying there trying to decipher the pattern printed on the wallpaper, but I can't make sense of it: moons, archways, something or other whose corners ought to overlap but have been left open, I can't make sense of what I'm looking at. I shut my eyes. She'll feel better once she's slept, my mother says. The light in my room is dim because the blinds have been lowered, but if the window were open, I could raise my eyelids and see the burning mountains from my bed, could peer through my window as if through a magnifying glass at the huge red and blue shimmering rock formation, this motionless beast on the horizon whose thirst has gone unslaked for centuries, not even moss can grow on it. Or have my eyelids themselves become heavy curtains blocking my view of this fire that has turned to stone. Oh, not at all. Just try taking a stroll all the way across the city and then through the city's outskirts, which used to be desert, and then through the desert itself all the way to the mountains. Or else it's nighttime. She's burning up, my mother says. The mountains don't burn at night. Watch out, it's hot. Only between two and seven. When the sun's on its way downhill. I could gaze at a chair, a table, a door. But the mountains are too much for my gaze to hold, they are bellowing and bursting my eyeballs. Do you think she's in pain, my mother asks my father. Now the animal is rending my hair with its stone teeth, tearing out huge chunks of it, even your own mother won't recognize you, eye sockets empty, the skull hairless, nice and cool, at last I am seeing the fire creature up close. I don't think so, my father says. In my blindness I can finally see that this creature intends to drink me dry. Would you call the doctor, my mother says to my father. She places a cool cloth on my lips. How long do you think the Difunta Correa lay in the desert before they found her. I don't know, my wet nurse says. Hours. Or days. At night it gets cold in the desert. Yes, she says. Pink room for a girl. Home. At home.

Well, young lady, says my father's friend, the doctor who is standing beside my bed when I wake up. Now we're going to cook the goose of that fever of yours. Open your mouth, he says and shoves a spoon containing a bitter liquid into it. *Bumped his head as he went to bed,* I can hear somebody singing. The doctor is a tall man with a hairless skull. His mouth keeps smiling as he pours his medicine into me, but with his eyes he's watching to make sure the medicine disappears completely inside me. *It's raining, it's pouring*—and then comes the snow. My grandmother is the only one in the family who can still remember snow. He puts one hand on my forehead, nods in my mother's direction and says, she'll be fine again in no time. My mother says she's sometimes heard me talking to myself even without a fever. What was his opinion of that? It's a stage children go through, says my father's friend, the doctor, girls especially. And he snaps shut his bag in which he keeps his implements and medications. *Couldn't get up in the morning.* My mother says to me: You'll see, any minute now those nasty bacteria will give up the ghost. The doctor says: They're already thrashing about and gasping for breath. My mother says: And they're screaming for help, but no one's going to help them, you'll see. But, I say. I can hear the singing inside me. No buts, the doctor says, you'll be fit as a fiddle in no time.

I am lying in bed, and in my body the goose of my illness is being cooked, what goose is that, our housekeeper is vacuuming, and when it's quiet I know she's still there all the same, she's polishing the mirrors, cleaning my piano down in the living room, scrubbing a sink or a tub, putting clean sheets on my parents' bed, ironing. Or else. She's gone out after all, to do the shopping, pick fruit in the garden. My forehead is cooler than during the night, I've burrowed deep into my pillow and lie there, eyes open, gazing at the garlands of roses printed on the wallpaper in my room, I can recognize the roses as roses again, I am trying to distinguish the silence of being alone from other silence. Around noon I hear noises down below, the housekeeper is setting to work in the kitchen, stirring, blending and chopping, icebox open, icebox shut, she is making lunch for my mother and me. I don't feel like eating. The goose. In the afternoon there are dishes to wash, far in the distance I hear plates clacking together, the sound muted by water and suds, and in the silence that follows I know the washing machine is being filled with dirty laundry, shortly afterward its drum begins to revolve, I can't keep my eyes open, an hour or two later the machine wakes me, wailing and vibrating in its spin cycle, then everything is silent once more, the housekeeper carries the laundry out into the garden and hangs it on the clothesline in the fresh air.

Ever since our housekeeper's husband went away and her son, as she says, struck out on his own, she's been sharing an apartment with her father-in-law. The two of them were what remained behind. So to speak. As the housekeeper says. The housekeeper says: My father-in-law can't walk so well anymore. He needs a cane. Or she says: I definitely want to see this movie with my father-in-law. Or: My father-in-law doesn't like potatoes. When she says anything at all. Sometimes she smiles when our paths cross in the house. When I ask my mother where her husband is, my mother says: One doesn't ask such things, it's none of our business. She could marry her father-in-law, I say. It's none of our business, my mother says. By the time you get married, everything will be all right again, my father said to me, standing beside my sickbed. How old is she, I ask. About my age, my mother says, and then she says: No more questions. Oh, I say, I thought she was an old woman already. I don't want to hear another word about it, my mother says, and points to my math textbook with her pen. I look at my math book and don't say anything else, but I am thinking that our housekeeper looks much older than my mother, she looks old enough to be my grandmother, and her bones are very brittle too. All she has to do is stumble to break her foot, and when she knocks on a door too energetically, her wrist-bone splinters. She says it's called bones of glass when a person has bones like that, and since parts of her are always shattering, she's often out sick, and then my mother has to do all the cooking, ironing and cleaning herself. A squared plus B squared equals C squared. I try to imagine how transparent our housekeeper is on the inside with all her glass bones. If she never remarries, when will everything be all right again. Will things just go on like that until she's broken into a thousand tiny particles and has to be swept up with a dustpan and brush, on and on until everything will never be all right again.

That the child survived has to be a miracle, I say to my wet nurse. We're on our way to the market hall, she's letting me carry the basket. Besides us there isn't anyone at all on the street. Of course it is, my wet nurse says. The side of the street we are walking on lies in the shade of the buildings. If the mother had survived too, it wouldn't have been a miracle. No, my wet nurse says, probably not. Then it would just have been a difficult journey. Probably, my wet nurse says. We have the sidewalk all to ourselves, block after block. They would simply have gotten where they were going eventually. Yes, my wet nurse says. So it's only because the mother died that there was room for a miracle. You can't look at it like that, my wet nurse says to me. We turn the corner to the left and find ourselves in bright sunshine. The air's so hot it's turned to liquid. An old woman comes toward us holding dozens upon dozens of empty plastic bags, white, pink and orange, that are puffing up in a breeze I cannot feel and rustling, the entire woman is puffed up and rustles as she walks,

I half expect her to flap these inferior wings and sail into the air before she reaches us. But she just brushes past us with all that emptiness clutched in her hands and laughs in my direction, she even looks back at me over her shoulder to give me the chance to gaze at her longer. And Jesus is dead too, I say. Of course, my wet nurse says. A few meters more, then we step sideways out of the heat into the gossipy shadows of the hall, which is packed full of people.

It's perfectly fine with me, the teacher says, if you have lots of lights on in the room you're in. But please turn off all the lights you aren't using. We nod. My lower arms are lying neatly one atop the other. Save electricity, the teacher says. Think of our country. Just look at yourselves, the teacher says, you have on clean clothes, you go to school, you have enough to eat. But these things don't come about automatically, the teacher says. This here is just a beginning, he says, imagine there were only water all around us. My father knows all about currents. If all of us work together, we can create new land using the sand that washes up, the teacher says. And all the people who will live on this new land will be just as well off as you. We nod. But the sea is treacherous, he says, and what we manage to wrest from it here might well be taken away from us someplace else. Have you ever seen the sea crashing against the cliffs? We nod. An island needs cliffs to keep the sea from sweeping it into the sea. Cliffs day in and day out. And do you know what it looks like beneath the sea? We shake our heads. Do you know what monsters live at a depth of four thousand meters? We shake our heads. It isn't possible to know them, the teacher says.

Do you hear that, Anna says to me during recess when a shot rings out behind the red brick wall surrounding our school-yard: That was my sister. We can't see anything. We wait for what will happen next. Now it's his turn, Anna says. Whose turn, I ask. The one who's in love with her. But only if he has the courage. A second shot rings out. We won, Anna shouts. Who won, I ask. He and my sister. Did they rob a bank? No, she says, it's something completely different. What sort of thing, I ask. Love, she says. If everything went well, both of them are dead now.

The Mazurka in F minor is the last piece Chopin wrote. They found it on his deathbed, my piano teacher says. My piano teacher always draws the curtains when she's giving a lesson so that of the sunshine outside the window all that makes its way into the room is a sulfurous light, this sulfurous light comes to rest on the piano keys, making them look like the worn-out teeth of someone who's smoked too much all his life. Besides the piano, the room contains a few chairs scattered about and a desk whose top is scratched. Some of the desk drawers are ajar, you can see there's nothing in them except for one which has an empty, wadded-up milk carton stuffed inside; the room smells of the milk's sour dregs. Milk. Drink. The place where I go for piano lessons is a public music school. The floors are linoleum-covered, the walls lined with soundproof insulation. The wastepaper basket is overflowing, and between the windows hangs a photograph of snowcapped mountains. My grandmother is the only one in the family who can still remember snow. Everything in the room—desk, chairs and piano—is somehow off-kilter. All the rooms in the school are like this, my lessons take place now in one room, now in another, one-hundred-seventeen, one-hundred-fifteen, three-twenty-eight, two-hundred-eleven, there are three entire floors of these rooms branching off the long corridors, and if it isn't mountains covered in snow, it's a big lake so big that nothing is reflected in it, and if it isn't a milk carton, it's a ball of crumpled-up music paper, and if the soundproof insulation has a hole in one spot, you can hear how, in the next room. How in the next room. How in the next room someone is playing the

Mazurka in F minor, Chopin's last composition, which they found on his deathbed.

Indistinguishable rooms, each just the same as every other one, *how sour sweet music is,* at the auditions for this school a girl with red hair sang a song I didn't know, we were free to choose, to sing anything we felt like, and the song this girl felt like singing resulted in her being expelled from the room. I'd picked the song of our homeland, my and my father's song. This school is a gift, the woman overseeing the auditions had said as she was signing my acceptance form, a gift from whom, I'd wanted to ask but didn't get a chance to, a few students here, the woman went on to say, are ungrateful and fail to understand that a person is responsible for gifts he is given. But it is also true, I wanted to say later, when I was already familiar with the lopsided furniture and the yellow wool curtains and the smell of sour milk: No one is at home here, and at night the school is all alone. If you ever see anyone damage school property or leave trash behind, the woman had said to us, come tell me. But no one going into a room in this school ever sees another person, I thought to myself later, and the only time you hear anything of the other pupils is when the soundproof insulation has a hole in one spot, there's never anyone in sight, the corridors are always empty, and all the rooms look just the same. The trash is always there already, along with the lopsidedness and scratches. Maybe there aren't even any other pupils besides me. I'm supposed to tidy up the school one room at a time. It's certainly possible. Only a person who appreciates beauty can make music, the woman said that day as we sat around her in a circle. I never again saw anyone from this circle at the school. But my teacher doesn't say a word about this. In any case, it wasn't me who wadded up the milk carton and stuck it in the drawer, I say to her, and she replies: I know. Even my teacher is always just sitting in a chair beside the piano when I come in, she is waiting for me, and as she waits she leafs through her sheet music, the part in her hair is reflected in the gleaming black of the piano. My piano lesson is never cancelled, and the teacher is always there before me, she is always already sitting there, waiting. She too pays no attention to anything that might, behind her back, be standing open, scratched or starting to smell rancid. And even when I shut the double door behind me, she doesn't get up. She just nods in my direction and smiles, and her prominent cheekbones turn her eyes into slits, I shut the double door behind me, she says Hello and shakes hands with me when I have reached our instrument, without getting to her feet. So it must be better, I think, just to leave everything the way it is. Let the school spend the night all alone. Let anyone who wants go around at night spilling milk. I play. Press the keys down as deep as you can, my teacher says, and go even deeper once the note has sounded, it makes a difference. Keep your little finger on its tip, and change the pedal cleanly. Staccato. Count to yourself. When the same note is to be struck more than once, change fingers, but make each attack exactly as strong as the one before. There's a different photograph of our country hanging in every room, the woman overseeing the auditions had told us that day, but I have never seen mountains capped with snow, neither from my window nor on any trip. Our country is larger than you can imagine, the woman says, some day you too will see snow.

When my mother picks me up from piano lessons, I go hopping beside her from island to island across the city's stone carpet patterns: on black, white or gray. Those who. Then their friends. The ones who remember. Who are afraid. And finally everyone. Why can't I ever go home all by myself, I ask my mother. Because you're still too little for that, she says and takes my hand to cross the street. First look to the left to see if a car is coming, she says, and then to the right, and if nothing's coming, hurry across.

What's your name, where do you live. When I open the door to my room, it scrapes the wood in one spot, the floor in that spot has been marked in a semicircle by the opening door, but out in the hallway the floor is made of stone, stone that was once sand at the bottom of the sea, you can still see curved and spiral-shaped shells in it, but now it's hard and the shells are fixed in place and flat, the stone has been cut into slices slab after slab, there's a sweetish smell in the bathroom, the smell of powder, my father and mother put a little in their shoes before they go out, if you turn the faucet too far to the left, the water comes out of the pipes boiling hot, be careful not to burn yourself, my father says, take the hair out of the comb after you comb your hair, my mother says, when you hold the toilet paper up to the light, it looks almost like milk glass, I wash my feet in the bidet, what's your name, where do you live. So-and-so. One-A, Such-and-such Street. When I go down the curved staircase, I always keep to the outer edge, the steps there are so wide there's room for my whole foot, close to the center I might slip, my mother explained and said: Be careful, and took me by the hand when I was still little, and when I want to unlock the lower part of the sideboard, I have to turn the key once to the right, but when I want to lock it, twice to the left, I'll never understand that, in front of the fireplace is a little brick platform covered with turquoise tiles, if I want I can set up shop there and sell paper fruit, or else lay my doll there. So-and-so. One-A, Such-and-such Street. Who used to live in this house, I ask my father. A person who got up to crooked business involving money, my father says. And the house was full of cats. House. Home. At home.

I see a long hallway with a room at the end that is my room. A bed and chest of drawers, and high up on the right is the window. Dreaming of a witch with an axe in her hand, I clamber over the fence to join Hansel and Gretel but then fall out of bed. Backward. Back to the endless hallway stretching on and on into the distance, now there's a woman sitting on the floor, upon her knees a rug that's been cut into strips, she is sewing them together end to end. To cover the hallway floor, she says. The bumpy wooden floor that vanishes in the shadows before the door to my room. Further back. To the left, my parents' room. My parents are nowhere to be seen. The door is standing open. Inside, a black leather sofa with a visitor seated on it, a woman I don't know. Further. On the wall to the right, the kitchen light switch. A figure sits atop the switch, encircling it with wire legs, a skinny man with glasses. I can't yet reach the switch. In the kitchen, a table, and on the table, a dirty teaspoon lying facedown. A banquette surrounds the kitchen table. I flip up its lid and see shoes. I bump into the table, the spoon falls to the floor with a clatter. Out of the room, moving backward. Further back. A mop leaning against the wall. The washrag hanging from it is still damp. And finally one last room just beside the front door, to the right or left I couldn't say, a room that's all lit up, someone sits there writing. Then my back thumps against the door, the big white door through which you enter.

And then comes the evening when I am left alone, I want to go to the neighbors' but can't find my way, in the stairwell I am suddenly standing at the foot of a ramp made of concrete that doesn't lead anywhere. I stand there waiting. Was that a dream, I ask my parents. Of course, they say, or do you imagine we would ever leave you all by yourself? And what sort of concrete is that supposed to have been? my mother asks, not to mention: What stairwell. I'm not sure, I say, but it was definitely a ramp made of concrete, I was standing at the bottom and it was nighttime. And what neighbors. I don't know, I say. But in the stairwell it smelled of fish. When did you dream all this? my father asks. A long time ago, I say. There, you see, he replies, when you're a child, you can't yet tell the difference between dreams and reality. He takes me in his arms, my mother laughs and goes into the kitchen. My parents have plenty of room. But I don't, not really. The head I inhabit was already furnished with other people's dreams for as long as I can remember, it seems to me. So then I fall down from time to time, or else I run into something, or get stuck. Father, and mother.

You play beautifully, says the young woman leaning against my piano. The young man is sitting in the armchair beside her, one leg crossed over the other, wagging his feet in time to the music as I play. He is staring off into space and appears to be waiting in no hurry at all for something that's about to happen. I used to like to sing, the young woman says. What I liked about it was that you can express anything you want without there being anything to see. Or touch. It's always only the air moving. You can even sing, she says, without there being anything to hear. You can sing on the inside. Do you know what I mean? Yes, I say. Do you like to go to piano lessons, the young woman asks. Yes, I say. Time for dinner, my mother calls from downstairs. I have to go, I say, nod to the two people and leave the room. When I open the door, it scrapes the wooden floor in a semicircle. Out in the hallway the floor is made of stone.

We wanted our daughter to learn an instrument, my father says to his friend. The friend has a pointy white beard which holds his face like a bowl made of hair, the bowl nods, making the face nod along with it, and the man says: Yes, that's good, and sticks a new bite of food in his mouth that he speared on his fork as my father was talking about me. She's taking piano lessons, my father says. My father doesn't say: Our daughter is learning how to set the air in motion. An instrument. I press a key, and the air starts moving. In the piano case standing upright before me, my teacher's eyes are reflected, and my own as well. I have no idea what's going on inside. Inside the case, the pressure of my hands is being transformed into the Mazurka in F minor, the piece that was found on Chopin's deathbed. The fork is no doubt an instrument as well. While the man, my father's friend, is now chewing, his beard moves up and down. Was Chopin just lying there with his mouth and eyes open, still holding the music paper in his waxy hands? Probably, my teacher says. Head scrapes paper, paper cuts finger, finger twirls the air, air, head, music. After dinner the man with the beard lays his napkin to one side and gets up from the table to smoke a cigar with my father in his room. The meat has been transformed within him, inside his body, into getting up and walking, I can't see from the outside exactly how, his shirt doesn't even show me my reflection, it has a checked pattern. A person has to eat, my aunt says. Meat, vegetables and bread are transformed into walking, coughing and laughing, into skin, eyes, fingernails and hair, the body itself is an instrument playing itself. You have to eat if you want to set yourself in motion, you don't have a choice. And drink as well, if you want to keep your mind clear, my aunt says. Through the closed door comes the smell of tobacco. Yes, drinking is important, she says to my grandmother. And when my grandmother isn't there, she says to my mother: It's happened before that she was disoriented because she hadn't drunk enough. Our daughter is learning to play an instrument, my father says. The music itself I cannot grasp.

A tiny house. It doesn't even reach to my knees. It's open in the front, you can look right into the ground floor and attic. On the ground floor, three Difunta Correas made of plaster are lying in a row, each with a plaster child at her breast. The paint that has made their clothes red or blue is already flaking. In the attic several jam jars hold flowers. And where the saint's garden ought to be, in front of the house, a few bottles have been stuck in the earth, filled or half-filled with water and screwed tightly shut. The house doesn't have to be any bigger because the Difuntas are never getting up again. And their children won't grow either, at least not on this altar. I ask my wet nurse: Do you think in real life the child is now old and gray? Maybe, my wet nurse says. Or maybe has grandchildren already? Maybe, my wet nurse says.

The tiny altar before which we are standing was built next to a bus stop in the dusty grass. My wet nurse discovered it on her way home, she wanted me to see it, as this was an example of a place, she said, where the saint and her child are finally in the shade.

At a bus stop on the way home, a woman gets on by the front door, followed by two men. As if in a dance, they pass her in the aisle to the right and left, the bus is still standing there with its motor running, waiting, the woman sees the men and at once tries to turn around and run back out the front door, but the men grab her by the hair, the woman begins to scream, the men drag her toward the back of the bus by the hair, and when the screaming woman now falls down, trying in vain to find a grip somewhere with her hands, and is dragged past us, her limbs contorted, my wet nurse starts shouting: Not by the hair! For pity's sake, not by the hair! But the men seem not to hear what my wet nurse is shouting, and then I see how this woman, who doesn't want to follow the men and therefore has stopped moving her feet but is nonetheless inextricably joined to her hair, falls out of the bus through one of the back doors right into the arms of the men, who have gotten out before her, and only now does the bell ring, giving the usual signal that the bus is about to depart, to warn anyone who might be intending to get on or off of the closing doors, the sound of the bell mingles with the woman's screams, which become fainter and eventually inaudible as the bus shuts its doors and resumes its route. Only then do I notice that blood is dripping from my nose onto my pink checked dress, my wet nurse says, we'll wash it out when we get home, with cold water.

On the way home, I tip my head back and try to stem the flow of blood with a handkerchief, I look up and see the sky, my wet nurse is leading me by the hand to keep me from falling, she says:

Careful, a curb, wait, there's a car coming on the right, here's a little dog. I know that beneath my shoes is the smooth, shiny pavement of the city in which I live, stone islands: black, gray and white, but all I see are clouds, distant water drifting past, it almost never rains here, my wet nurse pulls me to her by the elbow and says: Watch out, a beetle. I stare at the sun, blind today to the large, steaming cup that has been set into the ground here, a mosaic of paving stones on the sidewalk of the big street on the rounded corner where the café is, just a few blocks from our garden. I hear the voices of the people sitting here, hear them turning the pages of their newspapers, my gaze burned white by the sun. We turn to the left. Radio music is coming out of the shop where my mother always brings shoes for repair, I know that the metal roller blinds have been let down, see the sky and know that the shop is nonetheless open and that the owner is sitting in its most shadowy corner at a large machine that smells of oil, waiting for customers. I see an airplane high up in the sky, see it before I can hear it, see the white streak it carves into the blue, my parents are up there, they're on their way to Alaska, or: That's my mother's airplane, she's traveling to Rome, or: Today my father's sitting in that plane up there, he's flying far far away, where's he going, really far away, well if you don't even know where he's going then it can't be true, yes it is, my father's even flying across the ocean, well so where's he going. Mangos and oranges and strawberries, a sweet smell, for ten paces the sky is closer to me and bears green and yellow stripes, the awning is a roof for fruit and shoppers, the grocer cranks it out of the wall every day after lunch, or has the fruit already been spoiled by the sun, does it smell rotten, oh no, my wet nurse says, it looks nice and is in the shade. A few steps further, children are quarrelling on the steps of the ice-cream shop over a few coins, today I can't even buy you an ice-cream, my wet nurse says, and guides my feet to the right where it is quieter, our street. Before our garden gate, we detour around the man who is burning the grass from between the paving stones. I can't see the

piece of equipment he's using, just hear its hoarse flickering sound.
No, I say, but how about tomorrow.

When because of the blood still flowing from my nose my
mother holds my face under cold water until it turns to stone—my
wet nurse has meanwhile set to work on the pink checked dress—
but even at other times, when my mother rips a bandage from my
knee with an abrupt jerk, or combs my hair with a comb that gets
stuck in it and then says to me: Really, your hair, or when she
shows me how to pull a pair of thin stockings over my legs, pinch-
ing my leg along with the stockings, at such moments I'd like to
see her fall down the stairs or out the window, see her accidentally
stab herself while slicing bread. Whenever she says: It's just going
to hurt for a second, then it'll feel better, or: I know it pinches a
little, but you're a big girl now. You have to suffer for beauty, she
says. Beauty, beauty, a rat in your guts, your head in the cesspool,
beauty. Every time my mother hurts me, just for a second, a tiny
little bit, it won't last long, be brave, I always want to see her head
spinning away from me, reverberating with the good hard slap
I've just given her, and at last she'll be still.

Father, I say, they just came and took the woman away. We are
sitting on the living room rug, I am busy cutting the letters of the
alphabet out of fuzzy black paper for school, my father squats beside me on the rug, sorting the letters I've cut out into words. And
even though my wet nurse asked them not to pull the woman's
hair, they dragged her out of the bus by the hair. I see, my father
says. In the kitchen next door, Mother is frying things, washing
lettuce, stirring and chopping. What were you doing in that neigh-
borhood in the first place. The words LONG LIVE are written in
black on our carpet. It was because of the Difunta, I say. Who's
that, my father asks. A saint, I say, there's an altar to her there. I
see, my father says. Why do you think those men took the woman
away, I ask my father. Jealousy, he says, betrayal, love—they must

have had some reason. Do you think she's all right now? I'm sure she is, my father says.

Yesterday the railway workers tried to shoot out the tires of all the busses. The railway workers? I ask Anna. Yes, she says, didn't you hear the shots. Uh-huh, I say. So because of this it is forbidden, starting today, to travel by train. Oh, I say. Starting today, my friend says, there'll be a market in the station and on the tracks.

We could buy the shoes there, I say to my wet nurse. The shoe shop where we usually pick out shoes for her is closed today for technical reasons. In this shop, I always used to play hide-and-seek with Marie, my wet nurse's daughter, who in fact is my milk sister, behind the mirrors propped up at angles, while my wet nurse was pulling various shoes onto her bony faerie feet and then walking up and down a few steps to see which ones fit. My wet nurse stands for a long time studying the notice affixed to the closed blinds of the shop, which does not make it clear whether the shop is to be closed today only or perhaps tomorrow as well, but Marie has already seized me by the hand and is tugging me off in the direction of the train station.

When I see how shabby the station's cupola suddenly looks, I feel surprised at how quickly real life has taken note of the ban. Large pieces of cloth have been hung up to keep the plaster from falling on people's heads. Merchants have already set up shop in the ticket windows and on the platforms, they are selling handbags or scarves, candy, electrical cable, flowers and appliances. It is difficult to see the tracks between these piles of goods for sale, only occasionally does it happen that you are gazing at sneakers and watches and your eyes suddenly slip down into a gravel-filled crevice and off into the distance. You can still always just walk where you want to go. The shoes are inexpensive.

It's much faster to go by car anyhow, my father says. But: The smell of iron, the smeared windowpanes, the toilet with piss on the floor, when I flushed I could see the earth flying past beneath me through a hole, stepping from one car to the next, always with the fear the train might split in two, strangers putting bread and eggs into their mouths and audibly chewing, seats that could be transformed by skillful hands into beds, sleeping on the train, dreaming in the rhythm of the crossties, then waking up and being there already. When I get home, I'll have to get the old picture books down from the attic and cut out the locomotives, steam, conductor and all.

We have to drive far into the countryside to visit my father's parents. There never used to be altars beside the railway tracks because no one traveled on foot there. But from the back seat of the car I now and then see heaps of bottles filled with water, transparent mountains in honor of the Difunta. My mother says, how uncouth, unloading garbage in the countryside like that. My father says, it's time for things to be put in order around here. My parents hand me a bottle of water. I drink it. Car.

Once a year we go to visit my father's parents. We always spend four days with them during Pentecost. My grandmother has a high, rapid way of speaking, a child's voice, and for a long time I was convinced that every one of the little curls clinging tightly to her head was one of her words. My grandfather has a great deal of strength. When he says hello to me, he always starts by squeezing my hand in such a way that the ring I wear, a gift from my wet nurse, leaves bright red marks on the fingers to either side. Then he pulls me to him by one hand and wraps his arms around me, his embrace always makes me think of the machine belonging to the man who repairs our shoes in the shadowy corner of his shop, being embraced by my grandfather makes me feel like a shoe being inserted into this machine, and sooner or later, I assume, this rough treatment will tear the ears from my head.

My grandfather is a businessman. In the city in which my father was a child, I have never seen a single person who did not respond in kind when my grandfather greeted him. He's in real estate, my father says, and there's scarcely a building or piece of land here that did not at some point pass through his hands. It wouldn't be so surprising, I think, if my grandfather's hands, which grasp and release buildings and properties on a daily basis, were accidentally to tear off a little girl's ears one day. Do you know, my father's mother says to me with her curly little voice, I'm just setting the table while she reads the newspaper, do you know, she says, peering over the newspaper so she can observe me, how well-off you are with your parents. Yes, I say. You'd have to look far and wide to find parents like that, she says, and waits to see how I'll respond. I say: I know, and go to the cupboard to get out the cutlery. In the afternoon, when I'm just darting into the kitchen from the garden to get a drink, the living room door is slightly ajar and I hear my grandmother inside saying to my grandfather with her curlicue voice: There's something inherently spoiled about her, she'll always be like that, regardless of upbringing. And my grandfather's response: You may be right. Perhaps that's why he wants to tear my ears off, so I won't hear him and his wife talking about me in secret. On Pentecost, the disciples spoke to each man in his own tongue, my father told me as we were traveling to see his parents, by car this year for the first time. Each one of them was able to understand the word of God. And where was Jesus on Pentecost? Jesus had already died and been resurrected. What does a person look like when he's been resurrected, I ask. Just like always, he says, except now you can't grab hold of him. But ever since then languages have been separate again, I ask. Yes, my father says. I remember this conversation when I hear my grandparents speaking poorly of me through the living room door the Saturday before Pentecost.

The pews on which my father sat when he was a child are narrow and hard. Jesus is nailed to the cross up front. *In the beginning was the word,* the man standing in the pulpit says. My grandmother is gazing at the speaker, her eyes shining, each of her little curls wide awake, while my grandfather seems to be staring right through the wall of the church and grinding something massive with his iron jaws, perhaps he's clearing land in his thoughts. My father is holding my hand, my mother with her eyes the color of water is suddenly a foreigner in this nave, the innermost core of our nation, she lowers her eyes and during the entire sermon keeps them fixed on her blue leather handbag which is hanging from a hook beneath the shelf for the hymnal, a gift from my father. Up in front, Jesus is nailed to the cross. The man in the pulpit is telling the story of Creation, and if I understand correctly, what happened was that reality filled God's words to the brim with all the things God spoke of when he still had no one to talk to but himself: The trees grew into his word tree, the fish swam after his word fish and quickly slipped into it between scales that were already there from his speaking of scales, the birds darted up to the sky, following the feathers God had already proclaimed, and pulled them on over their heads, and Adam and Eve filled the words Adam and Eve with blood, bones, kidneys, intestines, heart, eyes and mouth and all the rest of what God talked about to himself when he was still alone. You'd have to look far and wide to find parents like that. Up in front, Jesus is nailed to the cross. Why does mankind have so many different languages? I ask my father as we are walking back to his parents' house hand in hand after the service. So now can anyone just come and take a word away from the thing it belongs to, I ask, or toss it over some other thing like a blanket, can any person who speaks be a thief? Can he? And what about a person who keeps silent? Do you need the word chair to sit in a chair? No, I say. Well then, my father says. And if a person says: I am sitting, and you can see he is standing up, do you need the word chair? No, I say. You don't have to speak of things you can grab hold of. But then what about the ones who were resurrected, I want to ask, but just then we reach my grandparents' house and my father is holding the door for everyone. There's something inherently spoiled about her, my grandparents said when they thought I wouldn't hear them. Perhaps it's because the railway has been abolished that you can no longer ride along the words as if they were tracks, always arriving at the same thing by the same route. Only recently, since we've started going places on foot or in the car, have I begun to notice forks in the road again, crossroads, or old and new roads leading in the same direction by parallel paths, and also regions that don't have any roads at all, but even then you can still get places by walking as the crow flies. Since the railway has been abolished, words can run away from their things in all sorts of ways, they can hide in the underbrush or the mountains. Trees, fish and birds stand in silence somewhere while someone who possibly has never seen them before is talking about them, or someone who has seen them neglects to bring them up. In front of the church, on the cross, Jesus is nailed. Pews, tablecloths, green twigs, Jesus on the cross, his body contorted, the pulpit whose roof is heavily laden with wooden fruits and leaves, the hook on which you can hang your handbag, shining eyes, jaws made of iron, my father's warm hand, my mother's eyes the color of water that she is trying to conceal, and Jesus, who always and everywhere, in every church, but also on the street, in public squares and courtyards, in rooms, corners, niches and above people's beds, is fastened firmly to the cross. God must have been terribly lonely before he began with Creation, otherwise a person doesn't speak to himself of kidneys and bones.

The Difunta walked right through the desert without a path, I say to my wet nurse when we're back from our Pentecost trip, the

two of us are walking on the shady side of the street, my mother's
sent us to the market hall to do the shopping. With every step she
was able to decide what direction to walk in, and still the only
place she got to was her own death. Meat, fish and vegetables, this
fresh and at the same time raw smell, and running beneath all of
it, an undercurrent, the smell of the rotten produce that is stacked
in baskets behind the hall in the mornings and collected in the af-
ternoons. She was free to choose any route at all, but nonetheless
she arrived precisely at the place where she would die, I say to my
wet nurse. Every time we come to the market hall, I look at the
leaves that have been torn from the turnips and cabbages, all soft
beneath my steps, already crushed black by other feet, and feel
surprised at how quickly it happens that something that was still
alive just a day before can turn rotten and smell. It was too long
a trip for her, but she couldn't know that beforehand, my wet
nurse says. Today I perceive the smell of rotting food more
sharply, today, it seems to me, this smell is overpowering that of
the living things, the freshly slaughtered meat and freshly caught
fish. If the desert hadn't been so endless, she wouldn't have
walked herself to death, my wet nurse says. Things could have
turned out quite differently. Everything you see here wants to be
bought, she often used to say to me when we went shopping in the
market hall, and then I imagined the fish, pieces of meat and vegetables calling out to the customers until each item, or almost
each, had been purchased. In this market hall I realized for the
first time that I live in a very large city. If there had been paths,
surely she would have encountered some other person who would
have been able to give her and her child something to drink, I say
to my wet nurse. We buy apples, grapes and potatoes. Not until
we are about to say goodbye in front of my house and she is hand-
ing me the basket does she say to me: Marie didn't come home.
She hasn't been home in three days. Before I can answer, she turns
around and leaves, and it seems to me as if I am seeing her back
for the first time. You forgot the onions, my mother says when I

set down the basket in front of her, didn't you look at the list I gave you.

My father takes me on his lap. I lay myself flat against his belly and curl up so that my head comes to rest between his head and shoulder. He rocks me back and forth, softly singing the song of our homeland, a song in a minor key, my and my father's song, we often sit together like this, but while he is really singing, I release my breath only on certain notes, as the desire strikes me, very softly. Sometimes my breath fits with what he is singing, but often it doesn't, and then the whole thing sounds off-kilter and clashes, but this too pleases him and me. I sing him my notes quietly against his skin from the outside, into his throat, while at the same time I am listening through shirt and shoulder to the blood circulating inside my father. Again.

Don't touch, my mother says, can't you see it's wild. The dog I want to pet has been trotting beside me ever since the café on the corner. He just appeared from nowhere, perhaps from the smoke made of stone coming out of the coffee cup set in the ground as a mosaic. The café has been closed for several days. Dog. Just look at it, it's filthy, my mother says. The dog remains at my side. It doesn't even have a collar, my mother says. It's true, the dog doesn't have a collar or a leash. Who do you think would take away even the collar and leash of a dog like that, I ask my mother. It never had a collar and leash, my mother says, you can see it was always wild, it just came to the city out of greed, to eat garbage. It should be put to sleep, my mother says. They multiply just like rats, she says, they come to the city, eat their fill, and then multiply like rats. I let go of my mother's hand and say to the dog: Sit! My mother says, come on, we have to go; the dog sits down. My mother says: Well, then don't, and goes on walking. Lie down! I say to the dog, and the dog lies down. I run after my mother, the dog obeys me, I shout, did you see that. Of course, she says, and takes my hand again. A few times I turn around to look at the dog, he is still lying there just where I told him to.

Why am I never allowed to go anywhere by myself, I ask my mother. Because you can never know what might happen, my mother says. We walk into the park at whose center a large man made of stone is standing. Besides this man, no one is here, but in a country where the sun is almost always shining, no one likes to go for walks in the middle of the day, not even in the shade. Or does everyone who comes here alone for a walk get turned to stone, I ask my mother. What nonsense, she replies and goes on walking.

You told your father about our outing, didn't you, my wet nurse asks me and smiles. She has come to say goodbye to me. Yes, I say. Just imagine, I say, he never heard of the Difunta. Well, he knows other things, my wet nurse says and smiles. Of course he does, I reply. My father knows all about currents. Let your parents know, my wet nurse says, tell them that even though I didn't know this before I am seriously ill and cannot work any more. What do you have? I ask. Tell them I have to look after my old father, who lives outside our city. Where does your father live? Tell them I think it would do you good to start finding your own way without me. I see, I say. Then she gets up, gives me a hug, still smiling, and leaves. When I look out the window to watch her go, I see the olive-colored handbag from which she one day retrieved the little card with the picture of the Difunta dangling from her arm, just the way it used to on all our walks.

Certain things are now being centrally regulated, my father says when I tell him that the coffee cup on the corner where the café used to be now has a beard of grass, as does the steam made of stone rising from it. As you see, he says, the café didn't make it. That's true, I think, for in the last few weeks before it closed, I saw fewer and fewer people sitting there. They were really cutthroat businessmen, my father says, or do you think people want to give an arm and a leg for a cup of coffee. The city will go to ruin, my father says, if individuals who think only of themselves are allowed to call the shots. The sentence spoken by the examiner at my audition for the music school occurs to me: Only a person who appreciates beauty can make music. And what about the man who always burns the grass away in front of our house? He's on vacation, my father says.

Other people have our piano now, I hear someone saying behind me as I am just about to shut the window because it's already so hot again outside. I turn around and see the red-haired girl who didn't pass the audition for the music school sitting on my sofa, her legs are dangling down and are still so short that even if this girl were able to play the piano, she'd never be able to reach the pedals. How come you haven't grown since then, I want to ask, but just then the door quietly opens and the housekeeper serves us cookies on a plate. I thought you girls would like these, she says and smiles, then she leaves us alone again. Even the table where I learned to write, the girl says. And my mother's crystal collection. When the girl stands up now to hand me the plate, there isn't even an imprint from her body left behind on the sofa, that's apparently how little she weighs.

Your father works hard, my mother says. No cars to the left, no cars to the right, then hurry across. We are picking my father up from work, just like every Friday. In the building in which my father keeps everything in order the grass is probably up to his knees by now. He's got to slash his way through with a knife, and when finally he's found order and wants to give it something to eat and drink, it lashes out at him, biting and scratching, order is ungrateful. There are many in this city who fail to appreciate beauty, many who do not value the gift that has been given them and allow the thing entrusted them to deteriorate. It's work to be human, my father once said, and I myself can see how nature reclaims everything that isn't defended against it day after day. To keep the sea from sweeping it into the sea. Certain things are now being centrally regulated, my father said, this is a transitional period, we are setting out upon new paths. We are going where no one has gone before us. A person who wants to sell his car parks it beside the road with an empty bottle on its roof. I know that the city's stone carpet patterns are beneath my feet, gray, black and white, I used to leap from island to island when I went out with my mother: Those who. Then their friends. The ones who remember. Who are afraid. And finally everyone. Always black or always white or always gray, holding my mother's hand. New paths. The grass has already begun to obscure the black, white and gray. Green. Now I can walk straight ahead, right through the islands and the sea. Setting out upon new paths, where no one has walked before. Where the grass is growing. My father knows all about currents. Work.

If my wet nurse were here now, I could ask her why there wasn't any grass growing in the desert where the Difunta was walking. After all, the Difunta too had chosen a path no one had walked before. Or had so many people already walked there that all the grass was trampled? Is that what they call a desert? But then all of them must have been gone already by the time the Difunta passed by, otherwise someone would have found the saint before she died of thirst. Wouldn't they have? My father, my father. In other countries in which there is a time of year when snow covers everything, a person whose job it is to keep everything in order might possibly be able to take a rest, but here, where the sun is always shining, everything is constantly growing, everything simultaneously blossoms, bears fruit and sheds leaves without pause. Except in the desert. In the desert my father could rest from his labors.

I'm so glad to see you, I say to Marie, my wet nurse's daughter. My mother never used to allow her to come to our house, but today I walk into my room and there she is standing at the window gazing at the mountain. I see Marie, and at the same time I look right through her at the mountain, and the mountain, for which the window-frame was always too tight a fit, now has plenty of room inside Marie's body. I pull a chair up to the table so she can sit down beside me, there's already a plate of cake there. Your housekeeper brought it for me, Marie says. But eating isn't so easy for me anymore, she says, and only now, when she turns around, do I see she no longer has any hands, they've been cut off just above the wrist. Marie sits down next to me and hides her incomplete arms in her lap as if she were ashamed of them. I don't know whether the shoebox with the hands fell on the grass or into the flowerbed, she says. When I go to stroke her head, there's nothing but air.

But if you prune them daily, they can grow to be two hundred years old, my mother says, taking the shears back from me against my will and using them to indicate her little trees which are no taller than a head of cabbage. Because they have to concentrate more on growing. My mother has never taken any interest in our garden, instead she has always collected these landscapes that you can place on the windowsill in large clay bowls, landscapes in which the boulders are the size of pebbles and the trees are all knotted and twisted because they can't go straight up. The resistance challenges them, my mother says. And because of this there is more strength in each of these dwarf trunks than in an entire forest simply growing without any help from humankind.

Think how hard things must have been for her with such a husband, and now this, my mother says to her brother, my uncle. The wife of my uncle, my aunt by marriage, says: If she sells her car, she can pay for the funeral on her own. We ought at least to offer to take her in, my mother says, after all she's our sister. She won't want that, my aunt says. My mother's brother, my uncle, says:

How awful it must have been for her, after all she was standing
right beside him. And nothing happened to her? I ask. Absolutely
nothing, my father says. A miracle, my grandmother says. My
mother says: Not a hair on her head was touched. So there was
room for a miracle again, I think, because this uncle who lived far
away and was married to my mother's older sister died alone. A
car went off the road and ran over him on the sidewalk. Perhaps
there was snow on the ground there, in the southernmost tip of
our country where I've never been. And that's why the car slipped
off the road. Our country is larger than you can imagine. The
driver was probably drunk, my grandmother says. My mother's
sister, my aunt who lives far away, had been walking arm in arm
with her husband, but only he was struck by the car and dragged
along the ground a short distance, then he remained lying there
and died. Knowing her, she won't even want us at the funeral, says
my aunt by marriage. My grandmother says: I'm going to go in
any case. I saw my faraway aunt, who is now a widow, and my
uncle by marriage, who from one minute to the next was snatched
from her side, on only a single occasion. The two of them came to
visit only once, for my grandmother's eightieth birthday, when
she'd asked to have all her children around her once more. I remember this uncle very clearly, he always said a great many things
which caused the other side—my mother, my father, my mother's
brother, my aunt by marriage and even my grandmother—to respond with a great deal of silence. I can't remember specifically
what this uncle used to say, just a single sentence that kept return-
ing again and again like a refrain and provided the conclusion to
whatever train of thought he was pursuing: And this is quite simply not true, it's simply not how it is, he would say from time to
time, and afterward would seem to be awaiting a response. But I
think it was precisely this sentence that always produced the silence on the part of the others, a silence that was new to me. The
wife of this very talkative uncle, my mother's older sister, was also
silent, but in a different way. She was silent at her husband's side

and thus seemed to be standing up to the silence of her relatives. Perhaps it was only because of all this silence that paid us a visit on my grandmother's eightieth birthday that I came to believe that my aunt and her husband, who now is no longer alive, had settled in a region of our country in which there is snow. Perhaps this really is why the car ran off the road. It certainly isn't proper to drink in the morning, my aunt now says, but my grandmother doesn't respond.

Anyone who wants is now permitted to shoot pigeons, Anna says, as a series of shots rings out once more beyond the walls of our schoolyard. Because they destroy buildings with their shit. That's a filthy word, I say. But that's the reason, Anna says. And dogs. The wild ones. Sit, I think. Lie down. They multiply just like rats, I say to Anna. That's stupid, Anna says.

Since my piano lesson was canceled today: The teacher wasn't already sitting on a chair at the piano when I came into the room, the part in her hair wasn't being mirrored in the shiny black of the instrument, she wasn't leafing through her sheet music and didn't nod to me, nor did her eyes narrow to slits, as her smile wasn't there, and so she didn't shake hands with me either, for I didn't even walk over to the piano when I saw there was no one in the lesson room, but instead remained standing at the door for a moment, then quickly turned around and closed the double door from the outside; since my piano lesson was cancelled today, I sit in the tall grass on the lawn in front of the building, waiting for my mother, who will come in an hour to pick me up, my mother uses the hour during which I have my piano lesson to get her hair done, or her finger- or toenails, or she lies down on a bench at the salon and gets a tan or a massage. In the middle of the lawn where I am sitting, amid the blossoming grasses which haven't been mowed for some time now, the gardener is on vacation, my father said, amid the stinging nettles and horsetail that are beginning to

take over, stands a man made of stone who must also have come
alone to take a walk here, I think, and I lean my back against the
stone leg of his trousers while I wait. The man is cold. But at least,
I think, he was turned to stone while standing up, so that even if
the grass were to grow much taller, you would still be able to see
him for quite some time. The Difunta died lying down. If she were
lying here with her child, it would already be impossible for anyone to find them.

You should be proud—after all, you know him, my mother
says. And for the first time I gaze up past the stone trouser legs,
let my eyes meander up the stone to the lapels and then to the face
that is so smoothly polished a blade of grass could never get
caught there and put down roots. And indeed: I see a bowl made
of hair that is now made of stone containing the head of the man
who not long ago was sitting with us. I think of the Difunta, think
of Jesus who everywhere, in every church, but also on streets, public squares and courtyards, in rooms, corners, niches and above
people's beds, is forever nailed to the cross, and I ask my mother
what the man died of in whose body our food was transformed
not long ago into walking and coughing. But my mother says he
isn't dead, he's coming to visit us again next Sunday, and then I
can ask him myself what it's like to be hewn in stone. I'm definitely not going to shake hands with him again, I think. Shake
hands, shake hands, say hello. I don't know whether the box with
the hands . . . So where's the miracle then? My mother says, forget about miracles, superstition can take you only so far, the main
thing is having a role model. As we are walking back through the
park, this time I raise my eyes at this end, too, where the other
man made of stone is standing, and let my eyes travel along the
granite placket of a lab coat and up to the head, when I was sick
the coat was white, now it's made of reddish granite, the head is
as bare as it was when I was sick, and polished smooth as a mirror, perhaps the bald head bending over my sickbed was stone

even then and the transformation had already begun imperceptibly from above. You are at home in this city more than others are, my mother says. I can see this. The city is starting to become our own stone dwelling, inhabited by my father's chiseled friends. Everyone should model themselves on these men, my mother says, but at our house they are regular guests. Is everyone who models himself on them supposed to become cold just like them? You are able to see them close up, my mother says, that's something to be proud of. On the median of the main street that leads up the hill, we encounter a third figure made of stone, one which has only recently been erected there. Its face has not yet been carved, but I consider it quite possible that just a few days from now the stone will have soft lips like the lips of a woman. Those who. Then their friends. Those who remember. Who are afraid. And finally everyone. Everyone everyone.

The teacher pulls a ruler out of Anna's pencil case, holds it up in the air and says: Down with the centimeter! And snaps the ruler in two. The smallest new unit of measure is approximately three and a half centimeters long. Electricity, too, has started coming out of the outlet at a faster rate. If a person were now to go on a journey, he would need adaptors to translate the electrical current, but why would anyone want to go traveling outside the country? Our country is larger than I can imagine. Before and Elsewhere are squatting one atop the other, copulating. How disgusting, the teacher says. Milk is now being sold in rectangular cardboard boxes that hold as much liquid as a bucket used to. The teacher says, why should a person go shopping every single day, what use is a mere liter to a large family. Lay in supplies, the teacher says. And then conserve your resources. This is true. But we, for example, are only father, mother and child. And my mother's brother and his wife are only man and wife. And as of recently, my mother's sister is all alone, a widow. She has surely already placed an empty bottle on the roof of her car to sell it in order to be able to cover the cost of her husband's funeral without assistance. That's an exception, the teacher says. In this country, in which the sun is almost always shining, everything is constantly blossoming, growing and rotting, and young women get pregnant again and again, Anna for example has five siblings, and even if the shooting the other day happened to go well and her sister is no longer alive, that would still leave four. Families like ours are the exception, the teacher says. Perhaps my grandmother brought this withering along with her from the place where my mother was an infant, her face gray and white beneath the woolen cap, brought this dying-out from that other world where for several months a year everything lies beneath a layer of snow.

You are our greatest treasure, my father says. You are our greatest treasure, my mother says too. This is one of those sentences where my parents cross paths as if at a busy intersection. Why don't I have any siblings, I used to ask my mother now and then when I was younger. There are children who have siblings and others who don't, my mother said. My father said: Things might change, you never know. I read somewhere, I say to my mother, that if you cradle a block of wood in your arms long enough and let your tears pour down on it, the block of wood can come to life and turn into either a brother or sister, depending. Who writes nonsense like that, my mother says. Neither my mother's brother nor her faraway sister, who surely has placed the empty bottle atop her car by now, produced children. But my mother is responsible for the existence of a child. The fruit of love. My father no doubt sat there waiting for me to ripen, then he plucked me from the tree and handed me to my mother, and she bit into me just like an apple. Or like . . . My father is responsible for the existence of a child. Things might change, you never know. My mother's treasure—me—has meanwhile been almost entirely eaten up, and there are no second helpings, or like . . . My mother is conserving me. Careful, it's hot. My father could keep plucking

apples from trees, since the land belongs to him. At least as long
as the tree still bears fruit. My mother: the one who boiled me for
preserves. My father: the trickster. Whom did the land use to belong to, I ask. A profiteer, my father says, a person who just
wanted to make money with his property, you ought to have seen
the garden, my father says, the grass was up to your knees. Now
the grass everywhere in the city is up to your knees, except in our
garden, where it is shorn low to the ground, my father has been
cutting it himself since the gardener left for vacation. And no one
had pruned the fruit trees in years. No one would have wanted to
eat the apples that were growing then, my father says, they were
small, pulpy and sour. Now not only the apples but all the other
fruits of our garden are juicy and sweet, my father plucks them
from the tree, then my mother cooks them down to make preserves and seals them in air-tight jars. Lay in supplies and conserve
them. You are our greatest treasure. My parents cross paths in this
sentence as if at a busy intersection. My father made my mother
the gift of a child. Or if need be, saw down the tree, chop it into
bits and cry a great deal over it. Careful it's hot. For there are
some who don't know how to appreciate it when they are given a
gift. Brother and sister. Neither brother nor sister. Neither. Nor.
Things might change, you never know.

Even the method of telling time is now different, we are told.
Clocks are made by people, are they not, the teacher says. In such
a large country as ours, he says, where here everything is blossoming, growing and bearing fruit at the same time as, in other, more
distant regions, it is freezing, snowing or thawing, the concept of
"spring" is simply a matter of convention. The only question, he
says, is what one wishes to remember and how often. I want to remember my birthday, for example, I say. One day out of all the
days of the year is my birthday. One day out of all the days of the
year is the day on which I was born. Good, let's take your birthday, the teacher says. Formerly a year had three hundred and

sixty-five days, did it not, he says. Yes, I say. And after three hundred and sixty-five days, you punctually feel in the mood for your
birthday. Yes, I say. And what do you do when it's leap year, the
teacher asks. Does your feeling persist one day longer? I don't
know, I say. And what would you do if you were to lose your cal-
endar or sleep through an entire day and you no longer knew
what time it was? Then my parents would come in with the table
covered with presents and the music box. I see, the teacher says.
But if your parents were to come into your room with the table
after only two hundred and fifty days, or not until five hundred
and twenty-seven, would you enjoy your presents any less? No, I
say. Well then, the teacher says. All these things are a matter of
convention. You cannot feel time, he says. Time has to be measured. Clocks, after all, are made by people and not the other way
around.

My father-in-law doesn't see well, our housekeeper says. Last
week he didn't even want to come to the movies with me, she says.
My mother says: I'm sorry to hear that. Our housekeeper says:
The sunlight is hard on him. What he likes best is to sit with all
the shades drawn, and he doesn't even listen to the radio anymore.
He just sits there. My mother says: The hallway needs mopping.
Okay, the housekeeper says, gives me a smile and puts on her rub-
ber gloves.

If my wet nurse were here, I'd ask her about the sun. Day and
night still exist, even here, in this country where at least during
the day the sun is almost always shining. Our housekeeper says
her father-in-law couldn't care less whether it's night or day.
When she brings him his breakfast, then it's morning, her father-
in-law says to her, and that's good enough for him. When a person stays sitting in the dark too long, the day has only
twenty-three hours. For example. That's what my father says. My
father knows all about currents. When a person is put into a

niche overnight that is sealed up in front with a door, in the morning he'll fall out like a board.

I'm sitting on the steps in front of our house, I forgot my key. The young man who listened to me play the piano not long ago is sitting next to me, smoking a cigarette. Do you like living here, he asks. Yes, I say. Sometimes it surprises me, he says, how little about a house is actually the house itself. You can see that when there are lights on inside, he says, and takes a drag on his cigarette. Basically, all houses are transparent, the young man says, but when you are sitting inside, you don't notice, probably because the furniture and the rugs and all the things hanging on the walls block your view of the air. I can't help thinking of the glass bones of our housekeeper, who wears her aprons tied ever so tightly about her waist. Perhaps it's the same with her: She'd be transparent if she walked around without an apron. When I see a house from the outside at night, the young man says to me, it always surprises me a little that it isn't collapsing with all the heavy furniture in it. In our house there is a great deal of heavy furniture, I think, the older I get the more there is, my parents have been collecting old furniture as long as I can remember, they say it's nice for things finally to be given a place appropriate to their quality, to have a home where they are valued. Walls are basically as thin as paper, the young man says, thinner than the shells of shrimp. You are our greatest treasure. The young man sits next to me, smoking in silence. Whenever the priest talked about Noah's ark on Sundays, I always imagined the rooms of our house: cupboards, highboys and gothic benches, chandeliers, rugs, mirrors and pictures that took refuge here as if from a great flood. Where did this piece of furniture use to be, I ask my father as he instructs the workmen carrying a white and gold armoire into our front hall. My father says: You won't believe it, but I found this one in a pigsty, it was being used to store the fodder. On top of the cupboard two angels are trumpeting. Before I am allowed to place my sweaters inside it, my mother takes a hand brush and dustpan and cleans out the shelves. Food for animals, she says, in a genuine Baroque armoire. All I can see is dust. And when a person wants to eat a shrimp, the young man says, he just peels it out of its shell. With his bare hands, he says. Pink-colored walls, and the pink already flaking. Alas, the young man says and now falls silent as he sees my father coming toward us through the garden gate, my father gives me his hand and helps me to my feet, then he kisses me and says: So were you very bored, that's all he says, he just goes on ahead to open the door for me, goes up the steps, walking right through the feet, knees and heart of the young man, who has remained seated there, my father unlocks the door and stands to one side to let me enter before him, then he follows and shuts the door behind us, now we are in the cool interior of the house. Outside the man is no doubt still sitting there smoking his cigarette, outside the sun is no doubt still shining, just the same as ever.

My little sister finally came home yesterday, Anna says. That's nice, I say. She went right upstairs, Anna says, to our parents' bedroom, to the wardrobe, and took the air pistol out of the compartment where my father always keeps his handkerchiefs. Our parents hid it under their linens so we wouldn't find it, Anna says. My little sister, Anna says, took the air pistol out of its compartment, held it to her head and pulled the trigger. How old is your little sister, I ask. She was seven, Anna says.

She didn't even close the door to the wardrobe first, she says to me. I don't say anything. And my parents still aren't home yet, she says. Why not, I ask. First they went on vacation with my little sister, she says, to the mountains, but then a volcano erupted and wiped out the roads, so they had to stay longer than they planned to. Then they stopped on the way back to visit our grandparents, and my father was attacked right in front of the house by a rabid wolf, he had to go to the hospital, and on the very same day he was released, my grandmother slipped and fell, and so my parents stayed even longer, my mother kept house for my grandparents for a few weeks and took care of my grandfather, and my father went fishing a lot during this time, he likes to do that, Anna says, there's a lake there, and he caught a pike, they put it in the bathtub still alive and my little sister tamed it, on command it would jump out of the water and back again in a big arc like a dolphin, and finally, when they really were about to come home, the news arrived that they'd won a cruise, a trip around the entire world, they had to board the ship immediately, and so they went straight from my grandparents' house with their packed suitcases to the coast, but first they sent my little sister back home to us. How long have your parents been gone now, I ask. A year or two, Anna says. Oh, I say, I didn't know. And who's been taking care of your family all this time, I ask. First my big sister took care of us, but after she fell in love, I did, Anna says. The Mazurka in F minor is the last piece Chopin wrote. And how much longer will the cruise last? No one knows, Anna says. The world is big, you know. Larger than you can imagine. Yesterday my little sister finally came home, she says. She rang the doorbell right when I got home from school. My mother forgot to give her the key. She didn't have any luggage either. She didn't even say hello, Anna says, she just ran right upstairs into our parents' bedroom, to the wardrobe, and took the air pistol out of the compartment where my father always keeps his handkerchiefs, it was hidden there, and she held it to her head and pulled the trigger. You heard the shot, didn't you, Anna says to me. And she didn't even close the door to the wardrobe first, she says.

Marie is giving the little girl a piggyback ride, you can do that without hands. They ride like that to the window and back again, many trips from the sofa to the window and back. My piano teacher is sitting at the piano, this time she's playing a humorous piece, playing it quickly, faster and faster, probably she's smiling as she plays, but her smile is not reflected in the shiny black of the piano, nor are her hair and shoulders, not even her arms, which are reaching far to the left and right to put some verve into the humorous piece, no, I see only the back of my piano teacher, and through it I see the shiny body of my piano, in which the reflected black and white keys are jumping up and down like mad, Marie begins to gallop, the little girl screeches with pleasure. The little girl looks so much like Anna that I didn't even have to ask her name when she walked into my room. She's tucked the air pistol between her belt and dress so she won't lose it on her ride. Finally Marie unloads her burden on the sofa and falls onto the cushions beside the girl. I'm thirsty! the two of them cry in unison, they close their eyes, laughing, and gasp for breath, but the music keeps going. I run down to the kitchen, everything's quiet down there, my mother is just pruning her kitchen herb garden in the clay pots on the windowsill, she says, why are you so out of breath, are you feverish again, I say I'm fine, our housekeeper puts four glasses and a bottle of mineral water on a tray for me. Finally a bit of life around here, she says and smiles. Uh-huh, I say. My mother asks why I need four glasses, and what sort of life . . . but at just this moment one of the clay pots cracks apart in her hands and she forgets what she was asking, she curses the soil that's fallen on the floor, the housekeeper goes to get a broom and I leave the kitchen, balancing the tray on my hand all the way up the stairs, always the outer edge of the curve, the steps there are so wide there's room for my whole foot, close to the center I might slip, my mother said when I was little, adding: Careful.

Early in the morning, as we are waiting for the sports festival to begin, the air is still cool, and the smell of jasmine drifts across to us from the dusty bushes at the edge of the field. But as soon as the sun begins scorching the field, one of the teachers fires the starter's pistol, aiming at the sun, you heard the shot, didn't you, Anna says, but the sun doesn't fall out of the sky. From the moment this shot rings out, our bodies are kept moving at a trot from station to station, from one piece of equipment to the next—sweat, drink a lot, complete the circle—from the moment the shot rings out, our bodies are being measured against one another in exercise after exercise. The capacity of our flesh to leap, run, balance, hurl, throw or be thrown is being measured, faster, higher and farther. Knees, arms, heels, thighs and tendons, hair tied back to keep it out of the way. My mother gave me tea to bring with me: sweat, drink a lot, tea without sugar. And fruit. Food is important for a strong mind in a strong body, my aunt likes to say. And what else? Is that it? Just food? *Why oh why did the banana start to fly?* When a head knows how far back it must bend in order to succeed in throwing the discus the hand is holding, does this make it better able to resist the knife about to sever it from its torso? And if not, what happens to the knowledge of throwing that falls out of it? Does it wind up in the basket along with the head? Or does it fly off and go on vacation? My father's up there. My mother. High high up. He or she is now on a flight to Rome. To Rimini. Or Hawaii. The teacher says a sports festival is for celebrating bodies. You have to celebrate holidays on whatever days they happen to fall. Why do holidays fall? Why oh why. *'Cause no one caught its yellow skin and dragged it down to earth again.*

When we run into my wet nurse on the street—I'm walking beside my mother to what used to be the grocer's shop to collect our rations, the market hall has been closed for months—we say hello to her, and the wet nurse too utters a greeting, and when my mother says to her that it's been particularly hot these past few days, she says: Yes. My wet nurse is wearing an olive-colored skirt and brown stockings, and her hair is now gray all over. Sand grates beneath my shoes, someday someone will have to dig up the mosaics if he wants to go hopping through the city on islands of stone, first those, then those, then those, and finally everyone, the sand has gotten caught in the grass that shoots up tall between the paving stones. You heard the shots yourself, didn't you. Why can't I ever go anywhere all by myself. The closed blinds of the shop where my mother once brought our shoes for repair are now dusty. In front of the café on the corner, the lock securing the blinds is already rusted. The street has shut its eyes and is quiet. Silence is health. Well then, my mother says to my wet nurse. The nurse says: I should be going. Good-bye, my mother says first, then I say it, then my wet nurse.

No. For once let me just set the holidays down and dance, take myself into my own arms and for once just dance, scoop my body from the pit into which I've fallen, spit out the sand, remove my heels from the iron blocks on which they've been propped awaiting the starter's pistol, and hoist myself out of the watery lane marked on either side by a row of corks, let me celebrate my body, but without measuring tape and stopwatch, without sense and reason, dance, move my limbs however the fancy strikes me, simply celebrate that there is something in the place where my flesh and blood are and not nothing, that's how the young woman put it when she came in and hugged me and I felt nothing at all of her hug, as all the others followed her, gradually filling up my room, when if not on my birthday did my flesh and blood belong to me, she asked and then she switched on a little cassette recorder and sat down on the sofa, good music, when if not today should I be allowed, today or some other day, what does it matter, one of all the days in the year is, after all, the day on which I was born, and in any case today we are celebrating my birthday.

This afternoon we are celebrating and dancing while my mother celebrates her own body, either sitting or lying down, celebrates it without moving, my mother always says it's getting to be time for me as well to entrust my hands, feet and hair to someone who knows what to do with them, today, while she is reclining on a couch in one of these salons, entrusting her body or parts of it to someone who knows what to do with them, or else lying down on a tanning bed so as finally to be at home on this shore of the world, to grow into this continent on which the sun is almost always shining, while my piano lesson is not occurring, as has been the case for several weeks now, we are dancing, we dance as my mother puts her body in strangers' hands, luxuriating, and my father is being visited by several men, such as the one whose head rests in his beard as if in a bowl made of hair, also the doctor with the bald head and one or two others as well who no doubt have also been hewn in stone by now and are keeping the city cool, we dance as my father is holding court and the first floor of our house smells of tobacco although the door to his room remains tightly closed, these stony men are holding stone, and therefore everything is perfectly quiet downstairs, for the housekeeper isn't there either, she's broken one of her glass bones again and is at home in bed, lying flat on her back, but not to celebrate her body like my mother, she is merely waiting for the glass to melt back together again, but her father-in-law is sitting at her bedside and objects to her letting the sunlight in, so the bone cannot mend and the housekeeper can't come back to our house, if the Difunta had broken a glass bone, it wouldn't have been long before it had melted back together in the sun, and while you can't hear a word in our house, and no one is washing clothes or dishes either, we are celebrating my birthday upstairs, and dancing because there has been something and not nothing where my body is for so-and-so-many years now, how many exactly doesn't matter, celebrating my birthday, although there are a good five months left before my birthday arrives.

Is this the new system for telling time, I'd asked the young woman when she came into my room without knocking, her hands filled with colorful balloons, but she hadn't replied, after her the young man arrived holding a cake, for a strong mind in a strong body, there were eighteen pink candles burning on it, even though my birthday is five months away and I'm only going to be seventeen, the young man was followed by Anna's sister with red ribbons in her hair, the air pistol stuck in her belt, and Marie without hands, it doesn't matter, one of all the days in the year, after all, is the day on which I was born. The young man placed the cake on my desk, the woman released the balloons to float around the room and put on music, and while the first guests to arrive were still giving me their birthday wishes, new guests were already squeezing into the room. Marie was the first to start dancing. Meanwhile the room has completely filled up with guests, all of them are dancing, they are laughing and dancing and speaking loudly with one another, my piano teacher has come, and even the gardener who has been neglecting his work for so long now, others I know only by sight, for example the cobbler from the shadowy shop on the corner, or the woman who had such long hair when she got on the bus that she could be dragged off by the hair, her hair is gone now, but she is laughing, and when she gets herself a piece of cake, and then another, and then another, I can see all the other guests dancing right through her body, and through the guests standing behind her I can see yet other guests. A boy who not long ago used to go to our school is dancing with Marie, and since she doesn't have hands any longer, he is holding her by the shoulders when it's time for her to spin around. A handful of children including the red-haired girl who flunked the entrance examination are racing back and forth, back and forth with Anna's little sister from sofa to window and from window to sofa and back again, they are balancing eggs on their spoons as they run, and it doesn't matter at all that the room is so full, for the children with their spoons simply run right through the bodies of the dancers, and the young man cheers them on and shouts bravo every time one of them gets to the other side without dropping the egg.

But my father doesn't come upstairs to celebrate with us, and everything is perfectly quiet each time I go down to fetch bottles of mineral water from the refrigerator for my guests, or orange juice for the kids, and later even a bit of wine, everything downstairs remains perfectly still, and my father's door does not open a single time. The footsteps of the dancers cannot be heard at all down here, not even the children screeching or the laughter, but no sounds emanate from my father's room either, as if my father and his visitors were petrified with astonishment at something as yet unknown to me; only from outside, from the street, do I hear something like the roiling of water in which there are a great many fish packed in so tightly they keep bumping together and the water is bubbling and seething with fish and brown from the mud stirred up by them, the water keeps rearing up in countless silvery bodies as if the water itself were a body, nipping at itself and breathing with a thousand wide-open mouths, and in this way, I assume, it is making this sound I have never before heard, that today is striking our house from the outside.

Come, my father says, taking me by the hand, we have to leave. My mother is already sweeping my clothes from the Baroque armoire into a bag. Am I to be nourished on this journey by animal fodder, or by dust. For a strong mind in a strong body. It is nighttime. I am standing at the foot of a ramp made of concrete. So are we going to our uncle's funeral after all, I ask my mother. No, she says. Perhaps this sound I'd never heard before really did come from the great flood, and now we are abandoning this house, which has become too cramped, to all the pieces of furniture, rugs and mirrors that have taken refuge here over time, we are locking the door carefully to save the chandeliers, gothic benches, oil paintings and blue-patterned porcelain, and are going outside to drown. Nonsense, my mother says. Or are we going on vacation to visit our gardener? My father says: You're going to see snow. So that's why we're departing in the middle of the night, so the snow won't melt beneath the sun before we get there. Exactly, my father says. Your mother is staying here, he says. Let her fall down the stairs in this house crammed full of objects or get squeezed out the window. You have to suffer for beauty. Before the hands of strangers who know what they are doing can go to work on my skin and hair, my father takes me away.

We drive until we reach the foothills. But before we can get out, the car is surrounded by footsteps, and we see men shining flashlights at us, hear them tapping at the glass with their hands in search of a window that's been left open, my father starts the car again and uses it to thrust the men aside, and then we drive as fast as we can until we reach a place where there are no more men and the road vanishes among the trees, and we keep on driving for quite some time between the trees. At some point we stop, leave the car behind in the forest and begin our climb in a place that has no path. When we look behind us, we can still see tiny circular lights swinging back and forth down below, drunken stars slowly attempting to follow us, and for a while we hear shouts as well. Then it becomes quieter. Completely silent. And eventually, at last, when we have climbed quite high, from one step to the next, there is something bright and cold underfoot. The snow line, my father says. When I turn around, I can now see the shimmering slope marked with the black holes we are making, the prints left by our shoes. As we continue to climb, I claw my fingers through the snow all the way to the rock and look back. Press the keys down as deep as you can and go even deeper once the note has sounded, keep your little finger on its tip, staccato. Count to yourself. When the same note is to be struck more than once, change fingers, but make each attack exactly as strong as the one before. The abyss on the other side is suddenly right before me, I'd almost gone headfirst over the edge, downhill much faster than up. This side, that side. Now come this way, my father says, pointing to the left. The path he is showing me is so narrow you can put your feet down only in single file, and from the way we came it slopes down just as steeply as on the other side, the valleys are invisible from here, they have gotten stuck somewhere in the night far far below us, where it is still too warm for snow. I can't walk here. You have to, my father says. Haven't you ever walked along a mountain ridge, the young woman asks me, she is balancing very skillfully, without slipping, on the steep slope to my right. No, I say. We have to, my father says to me. All you have to do is not look down, the young woman says, then it's perfectly easy. It's perfectly easy, I say to my father. You see, he says, and keeps walking in front of me without turning around. I keep my eyes on his heels.

Surrounding us is a room filled with shadows, its door ajar, the lock was already broken open before we got there, the door leads to a garden that's gone to seed, and on the other side of the garden, where the land slopes down steeply behind the bushes, is the sea. All sorts of other things lie beyond the sea. But just the way my father took the song of our homeland, which I'd always heard trumpeted out of loudspeaker boxes on the street, and made it small and soft for me and combined it with my breath, all the huge vastness we left behind us as we fled is becoming small and soft as well, and as soon as I reach my father's lap, it leaps into his arms.

You know, my father says, everyone who comes to us has to go through the same thing. There has to be some justice. Yes, I say, of course. We certainly cannot demand of one person, he says, that he tell the truth, and then not ask the same thing of another. No, I say. The most important things for starters, says my father, are heat, cold and wet. Heat, cold and wet. Because all the things a person's ever thought are still present in his flesh. To begin with, you have to soften the flesh. Heat, cold or wet for the body of the person who has committed an offense, and at the same time send his gaze down a cul-de-sac, my father says, that's how you begin to guide his concentration to what is most crucial. To what is crucial, the offense, to delinquency and deliquescence, the things that fade away and rot. Precisely, my father says, so we start off with heat, cold or wet, and then you've got to have at least panes of milk glass to block off the windows, if there are windows at all, or better yet, brick over any hole that might let in some light. Paradise was an island too, my father says. And the person on duty is God. Precisely, my father says. *Be present at our table, Lord, be here and everywhere adored.* And now, he says, there are various approaches to choose from. Good, I say. First, my father says, the body is anchored by the limbs or else hung up by them, on a cot or chair or hook, so that the places most susceptible to pain are easily accessible. For it is only through pain, my father says, that the truth can be brought to light in the case of obstinate subjects. Yes, I say. The best place to bring the truth to light is the same for both men and women, between the legs. Oh, I say. You are no longer a child, my father says. No, I say. But there are other places as well, my father says: the tongue, nipples or eyes, for example. Tongue, nipples or eyes. Also the nape of the neck. The nape of the neck. So now, my father says, when the body has been fixed in place and can no longer escape, you can connect one or several of these places to an electrical circuit, or else, my father says, take up a rod with current running through it and use it to probe, stab or beat the body. Probe, stab or beat. You've seen the iron rod I stick in the ground to drive out the earthworms, haven't you. Yes, I say. Don't stick your fingers up your nose. Imagine something like that, my father says. The electricity drives the worms out of the ground, and the stronger the current, the faster they come out. Anna's father caught a pike the size of a dolphin, do you think he used a rod like that? Probably he did, my father says. So once you've connected a body to the electrical circuit, the truth comes out of it like a worm. That's right, my father says. A strong mind in a strong body. How strong the food itself must be. My father says, if someone stubbornly insists on keeping silent, we have to turn up the electricity until his flesh begins to burn. Careful it's hot. Electricity is the best means to drive what a person knows out of his mouth. But what if someone doesn't know anything? But if you are in a room without an electrical outlet, tongs or a knife will work as well. Tongs. Knife. If the knife is sharp enough, you can cut all the way around the soles of a man's or a woman's feet, for example, and then peel back the skin. Each time the body is injured, the recalcitrant spirit shows its face a bit more. Tear out eyeballs or cut off anything that sticks out—ears, noses, hands, feet—crush nipples, twist the entire body or just individual limbs. Simple kicks can work as well, my father says, if you haven't got any tools handy. *Pattycake pattycake baker's man.* If one of them needs longer, take a break with a few vitamins, fresh water, and there's always a doctor in attendance, and then everything starts again from the beginning. Fresh pain in a fresh body. Does the man with the bald head first dispense vitamins and then strike his stony skull against the skull of the obstinate individual until it bursts? If necessary, yes, my father says. Cook the goose of. And in this way the truth comes to light? Usually, my father says. But there are some who refuse to speak even then, my father says. With them, you can forget about the body, you have to go to work quite differently. Strap husband and wife one beside the other on benches. *Man and wife and wife and man, both are part of heaven's plan.* Then a couple of our people on top of the woman who you know, you're not a child any longer. Who know what to do. Or make the husband scream, see above, and the woman is tied up next to him, and make sure she keeps her eyes open, eyes open when you cross the street, to see, or the other way round, and the same thing works with the delinquent's parents, when a person hears through a thin wall for two days, to hear, how in the next room. How in the next room. Hears his father screaming, he'll soon be gagging on the truth and happy to vomit it up. Wait, I say. With little children it's even easier, my father says, starting at a weight of fifty-three pounds they can withstand the electrical current for quite some time. To hear, to see. And then the parents suddenly start talking so fast and so much you can hardly keep up taking notes. Up to fifty-two pounds we do it the other way round, we make the children watch what's happening to their parents. And the doctor weighs the children beforehand? Exactly, my father says, he's always in attendance. *Lullaby and goodnight.* My little sister, says Anna, ran right upstairs to our parents' bedroom, took the air pistol out of the compartment, held it to her head and pulled the trigger. She didn't even close the door to the wardrobe first. So Anna's father and mother are on that on that that sort of cruise. Love serves us well, my father says. Suddenly something crunches underfoot. My grandmother is the only one in the family who can still remember. Your mother's father, your grandfather, whom you never met, used to toss children into the air on the other side of the world if they were small and light enough, toss them into the air like birds and then shoot them before their parents' eyes. Under fifty-two pounds? Exactly, my father says. *Lullaby and.* But stunts like that do absolutely nothing to advance the cause, my father says, because afterward the parents are even less likely to talk. I think we've reached the snow line. No, not at all, my father says, there are no limits to the imagination, even here, but after all our objective is to bring the truth to light. I, for example, was against sending your wet nurse her daughter's hands, but in the end that was still better than arresting the wet nurse herself. Don't you agree? Probably, I say. Better to give a warning first, to let her know where things stood. Yes, I say. And after all it did work, my father says, the wet nurse finally left you in peace, and yet she herself is still alive as far as I know. Yes, I say, we ran into her not long ago. There, you see, my father says. A healthy dose of fear never hurts, he says. Adrenaline, he says, is produced by Mother Nature when a person is afraid, to heighten one's awareness of things that can help one. That sounds nice, I say. What? my father asks. Mother Nature, I say. Precisely, my father says. It's just as I always thought: The windows of the palace in which my father keeps everything in order, sirens wailing, are just painted on, not a single ray of sunlight ever enters the building, wailing and flashing, and these rooms devoid of light are filled with the struggle between justice, truth and love. The sirens have been transformed into birds and have flown out of sight. My father has bushy eyebrows which, in contrast to the blond hair that grows on his head, are completely black. When he smiles, he always furrows his eyebrows at the same time, making him look simultaneously cheerful and concerned. Now that I understand what things are like in Paradise, I am happy that my father is so often on duty. Now I know I have no reason to fear for him. If you aren't for us, you're against us, my father says, and this corresponds to the words that shoot through my head just before my eyes fall shut, his thoughts tuck my thoughts in tightly, and with his lips, which are as soft as those of a woman, my father gives me a goodnight kiss. I fall asleep. From now on, sleeping is my job.

The only light flickering in one of the lounges for the palace staff comes from the television. The announcer curses, wishes, prays and bellows. The men see and hear. When a long shot of the north curve fills the screen, it casts its pale reflection on their faces where they sit smoking, hissing through their teeth when their favorite lags behind. On the straightaway, the race cars can be seen close up for a few tenths of a second, darker and more vivid. At the lower edge of the screen you can read who is driving, how fast, in which position and so forth. The men seated before the television have their backs turned to the part of the room that lies in shadow, where a few beings trussed up like packages are lying on the floor with hoods over their heads—essence, deliquescence—waiting for the truth to. One really has to drag the words out of you. Just a simple hook will work as well. Even a clothes hanger if that's all you've got on hand. I'm trying to remember whom or what we turned our backs on when we lined up for assembly. The school building occupied the only edge of the quadrangle where no one was turning their backs on anyone or anything, closing off this edge of the square, but on the three other sides where we were standing, everything was open, and so everything that existed lay at our backs, we were turning our backs on everything that existed as we followed the advancing color guard with our eyes, just as we'd been instructed.

And now, my father says, the question is what to do with the material. Case A, if it's still alive, he says. House. Home. Go home. No no no, my father says, for us there's no going back, only forward. Just as in Nature, my father says. Off to distant shores. That's my father my mother up there flying to Rome to Rimini to Hawaii. There was always a doctor in attendance, he says. And a chaplain, of course. We released them into Heaven, still sleeping, my father says, and the chaplain prayed for them before their bodies hit the water. *The cradle will rock.* A miracle, far distant, the angels plummeting from blue to blue, from high up in the sky to the sea, sleeping, plunging, and still holding hands; my mother and I are standing down below at the harbor observing this miracle, and many other people are standing there as well, pointing at the angels and crossing themselves. Naturally, my father says, you have to take into account that the warm water on the ocean's surface displays a quite different pattern of currents than the cold water at the bottom. Pick the wrong spot, and the material will fail to sink but instead will get washed up somewhere at the feet of some beachgoer, and that's utterly unnecessary. Utterly unnecessary. The Arctic and Antarctic water masses, which are heavy because of their low temperature, sink to the bottom, my father says, when they collide with warmer currents, and in this way, flowing at enormous depths, they can reach all the way to the equator. All the way to the equator. Precisely, my father says. My father knows all about currents. But in order to take advantage of this effect, the flotsam must be cast overboard above the plateau of the ocean canyon situated at a depth of nine hundred and in parts up to one thousand three hundred meters below sea level. *Mirror mirror.* If, on the other hand, one discards something above the continental shelf, too close to the coastline, my father says, the warmer currents will cause it to drift along the shore, and it might well put down roots again a few towns away. And that is utterly unnecessary. No, I say, utterly unnecessary. When my father smiles, he draws up only one corner of his mouth, he entrusts one part of his face to the warmer currents. *The cradle will fall. When the bough breaks, the cradle will fall.* Then I smile as well. Then my eyelids fall shut.

I never would have thought there'd be so much music playing at the palace. From the outside, the building seems so quiet. Silence is health. Inside, though, people are ripping out other people's fingernails, you bitch, thwack, wham wham wham, *love is thicker than water, dance, stayin' alive*, and thwack, he's screaming his throat out, uh-huh, *stayin' alive*, and thwack, *night fever, baby come back, with a little luck*, into the cesspool with you, thwack, *too much too little too late, baby, the race is on, I can't let you go, and over again*, are you seeing stars yet, *love me please, just a little bit harder, I can still feel the glow*, heat, cold and wet, *I can't let you go*, give it to him, *and when you walk away from me baby, you're gonna be sorry*, you bitch, *together we can make it*, thwack thwack thwack, *no one knows who she is or what her name is, come on*, let's carve a flower in her right breast, in the left, in both, *let's go*, tell me what you see when you look on the dark side, *dance dance dance, so young to be loose and on her own*, tie her up by the hair, *hot child in the city, baby come back*, is black even a color, long live, *let's go, just a little bit harder*, put her on an iron bed, you, *you don't bring me flowers, you don't sing me love songs, you hardly talk to me anymore, when you come through the door at the end of the day*, a needle in the flesh, right next to the heart, it'll keep wobbling as long as it's still beating, a divining rod for the blood, a drum kit, drum it into him, beating, beating as long as the heart is still beating, *when I get home babe, I'm gonna light your fire, gonna wrap my arms around you, hold you close to me*, thwack, *I wanna taste your lips, I wanna kiss you all over,* shards of glass in your cunt, you old sow, *all over, till the night closes in, dance dance dance, it's easy to see when something's right and something wrong,* wham wham wham, thwack, wham wham wham, thwack, instruments made of metal in 4⁄4 or 3⁄4 time, it doesn't matter, just so it's louder than he is or she is, *love is thicker than water,* soften him up, him or her, with heat, cold and wet, bring her flesh to the melting point, then we'll see what's at the core, and then crack it between your teeth, crush it, grind it to dust, *stay with me, here with me, near with me, you're my one desire, dance dance dance, I need you babe, shadow dancing, three times a lady,* thwack, *follow me,* you bitch, *thicker than water.*

It all depends, my father says. For those who are already beyond sleep, Case B, there's always the classic variant, six feet under. Classic. With or without a stone. N.N. No Nonsense. No Needs. No Nothing. Nothing New. Nothing Natural. No Name, my father says. *In nomine patris.* What's your name, where do you live. So-and-so. One-A, Such-and-such Street. All just a matter of convention. Names, after all, are made by human beings and not the other way around. Of course, you can also sort according to the size and type of bones. The pits are then of corresponding size. But all in all it's easiest. And if there's no soccer field nearby, then just use a barrel filled with concrete, or else the foundation of some building. This too is a contribution to the development of our society, my father says, and looks simultaneously cheerful and concerned. Yes, I say. You were lucky that you were already here, my father says. And that I was on duty. Father. Mother. Ball. Car. From the very first moment I saw you, he says to me, I loved you. Lucky. If a person couldn't care less about children, then it doesn't matter to him, just so a mother with her baby or a woman far along in her pregnancy will still fit into a barrel. But children are our future. Lucky. I always knew that. And the future belongs to us, he says. That which is wrong will not survive. What is sick will die out, he says, just as in Nature. But the future belongs to us, my father says. And the future is our children. That which is wrong will not survive. What is sick will die out. But the future belongs to us.

Dumb man in the mountain, dumb child on his arm / Dumb the mountain, dumb the child: / Holy dumb man, bless this wound. To staunch the blood.

You needn't worry about the woman who gave birth to you, my father says. Her head was full of shit. That's a filthy word. And with all the other shit in her head, my father says, she forgot she had a child. Lucky lucky. A person who knows the laws and refuses to abide by them, my father says, has only himself to blame. And concrete, he says, is almost like amber, lucky, anything inside it will be preserved forever, forever, it's just that it isn't transparent, the concrete, and you don't hang it around your neck because it's too heavy. One corner of my father's mouth is being blown towards the equator.

I can remember the breasts of my wet nurse quite clearly. I drank from them a long time. . . .
Silence.

Your father had already been processed. Though at the time I didn't know he was your father. Just a trick of chance. Just the way chance sits in its iron chamber, making calculations. A person who is sleeping, by the way, falls more quickly. Sleep makes the body heavy. It's really true, he says. Funny, isn't it.

Our Father. Creator of Heaven and Earth, who, moved by your infinite fatherly love, have spoken to us through your own son Jesuschrist to show us the way to true happiness through your Gospel; your son who died on the cross out of love for us took our sins upon himself and showed us that all our sufferings hold within them the truth of salvation; and with his resurrection from the dead he gave us the certainty that one day all departed believers will rise up once more, Father, we who remember the departed Correa beseech you, grant us the presence of the Holy Spirit and favor us with your love, which looks so kindly upon us.

In return we promise to live day after day as good Christians, we shall uphold God's commandments, aid our brothers and love them with the same generosity and faithfulness as our unforgotten, departed Correa, in whom we have recognized the true meaning of Christianity.

For this we beseech you in the name of Christ our Lord.

From the very first moment I loved you, he says, and strokes my hair. Nothing is inherited, my father says. *Bone to bone, blood to blood.* That's all ridiculous. The way a child thinks is purely and solely a question of upbringing. Sorting. *Limb to limbs.* Your innocence, my father says. Have a look, says the young woman who has stepped from the garden into the room and is showing me her arm, on the inside of her elbow I see a small oval mole. I hold out my arm. On the inside of my elbow I see a small oval mole. You hadn't yet learned anything that was wrong, says my father, on whose lap I am still sitting, you were absolutely pure. Sorting. Three or four words perhaps. But beyond that, nothing. I could see it in your eyes, he says. That is why I loved you, says my father, from the very first moment. A child is given birth to by a mother, but is not part of that mother, praise God, he says. You were still free. Sorting. Father. Mother. Ball. Car. Through the young woman, I see the half-open door, and behind it flowers and weeds. And behind the flowers and weeds, the sea. Praise God. *Thus be they bonded.*

The young man is calling me, he wants to play ball with me in the depths of the sea, among the schools of fish and mussels.

Let's go, I say. But just as he is about to shoot the ball to me, his shinbone is caught in a current and goes swaying off, and when he tries to catch the ball with his hands, one of his hands gets caught in the algae, and while the other one touches the ball, it cannot grasp it because the little bones, each of them separately, are floating free, it is the missing flesh preventing the ball from being caught. The young man smiles at me, now it's my turn, I give the ball, which has slowly floated toward me all on its own, a push in his direction, the ball lands gently in the middle of the man's smile, it knocks the jawbones away from one another and lightly separates the upper jaw from the roof of the skull in which the imprints of veins can still be seen like a flower pattern, and so in the end it separates the smile from the smile.

When they find us, I am still sitting on my father's lap. At some point I fell asleep. On the lap of my father. They came in from the garden, or from the sea, to pluck me away from him, but that doesn't work, at first they just circle about, tugging at us, but in the end they realize they'll need a knife to separate us one from the other, and so they cut our arms through where they appear to have grown together, funny, isn't it? Now my and my father's tendons, muscles and all the blood are just lying there exposed. Everything is just as my father said it would be: They want to separate us one from the other and then take possession of your blood, he said, they want to pour your blood, doesn't one say spill, that may well be, or perhaps just drink it straight down, he said, but if they try to separate us, in the end all they'll have in their possession is at most the air that was between us, and the air isn't worth much, is it now? Nonetheless, my father says, or perhaps my blood will then flow like a rivulet through the separation, spill it and then something will grow, I've no idea, my father said, or else he said nothing at all, I think I've gotten things confused, my father merely held me on his lap a long time, a very long time, until finally I fell asleep in his arms, and he didn't say anything else, just sat there in silence.

It is written in my blood, they say, that my father is not my father, my mother not my mother and so on. The wood of the railing on which I keep a tight grip has such a beautiful dark gleam to it. Polished by the many hands that have already gripped it. I know, I say. With ninety-nine point five percent certainty. I know, I say. My father and my mother are standing trial here because when my father and mother, my father and mother, my father and mother . . . And then seized possession of me. Seized. I know, I say, of course. My father already told me everything. My name isn't. Yes. And my birthday presents too were on the wrong day year after year. Certainly. Certainly. On the table with wheels. *Plume in the summer wind, waywardly swaying.* But some day of the year is bound to be the day on which I was born, some day of the year is bound to be my birthday. Of all the many days of the year, some day that was there all along. Some word of all the words will no doubt be the last word some day, knife perhaps, or some other word, some word that was there all along. They show me photographs. The young woman. The young man. *Thus be they bonded.* Now I've been liberated, they tell me. That's good, I say. Liberated from Grandmother, who drinks in the morning, from the widowed aunt in a region of the country where snow sometimes falls, from the uncle who was struck by a car, from Grandfather through whose hands properties circulate, from Grandmother number two, who speaks two different languages, from woolen cap with pompom, wooden floor in which the door of my room scrapes a semicircle when it opens, from pink-colored house, smell of tobacco, Rose of Jericho, the dew in the garden, the salute to the flag and so on. Now I've been liberated from virtually everything. At the very bottom of the wooden toy chest lie a few crumbs, a rusted key ring and a broken crayon. Now they ask what I want to do now, now that my father and mother will have to go to prison and my father and mother have been dead so many years. Sleep, I say.

Don't talk with dirt in your mouth, she says to the young man and the young woman. She takes care of the house. She waits. When she visits her father in prison, he says: Don't forget, the future belongs to us. It's true that the ones made of stone have been toppled from their pedestals and carted away, but their roots continue to branch beneath the entire city. Just wait, it'll pass, her father says. They have no idea how to exterminate their enemies. Dilettantes, he says. Yes, she replies.

And to think I even paid her, her father says, and spits on the tile floor at his feet. He always repeats this sentence, spitting each time as well, when the topic of the housekeeper comes up, ever since the words natural born were used in court in connection with this woman. When she now walks past the palace in which until recently her father worked, she sees many of the people who walk past the building spitting as well. The only difference is that her father's spit is removed each day when his cell is cleaned, while the spit on the street before the palace in which her father used to work dries and leaves behind whitish marks, as if the spit contained a tiny bit of salt. You see, her father says, these days you can no longer trust anyone. No, she says. Since the visitors have stopped frequenting her room, there's no longer any need to serve refreshments.

Her father told her the truth, she says to Anna when she finds her standing at the door. Now she knows everything. Oh, Anna says. And, she says to Anna, she loves the truth. She loves the truth with all her heart, she says to Anna. And Anna, whose mother was an Indian and was trampled to death by horses but is currently on a cruise along with Anna's father, who was attacked by a rabid wolf but meanwhile is in the best of health again, while

Anna's sister had herself shot dead out of love, besides which the
volcano, the giant pike, and no one knows yet how much longer
the cruise will last: Anna nods and says good-bye.

As you see, her father says to her, I could just as well be lying
on the sofa at home reading. And it won't be much longer now.
Definitely not, she says to him. There just aren't enough of them
left. And the ones that are left still respect me, he says. She nods.

Now she always walks through the city all alone, and the city
is as good as empty. The traffic lights are working, but there are
very few cars on the road, and hardly any pedestrians at all. That's
not surprising, her father says to her, they just laze around the
house all day long, they have no idea what it means to work, they
sleep late, then they take a break for lunch, and after that it's already time to stop for the evening. That's no way to build a state,
her father says. Definitely not, she replies. The only person she
regularly encounters on the street is the old woman with the many
plastic bags puffed out with wind. She still walks rustling down
the street, looking as if it wouldn't cost her even a smile's worth
of effort to rise up in the air, that's why she always squanders a
smile, just like at their first encounter, by tossing it back over her
shoulder. The old woman was already old the first time she saw
her in the company of her wet nurse, and old she has remained. If
a person were to try to prick a hole in one of her bags, it wouldn't
improve matters but wouldn't make them any worse either.

What a difficult time they had toppling the men of stone from
their pedestals, she says. Because although the stone was just sitting on top, all the innards were made of concrete from the bones
to the kidneys, and the concrete was much harder than granite.
They really struggled with it, she said. Good, her father says. Finally they were forced to cart off all the concrete parts in one
piece. You see, her father says. I think I'm interested in the real es-

tate business, she says. Selling earth with air on top of it. Good, her father says. That's something you can live on.

The market hall has reopened, but with only a few vendors. One day the cobbler's blinds were rolled up again, and the large machine was carted away. A hairdresser took over the shop with the shadowy interior smelling of machine oil and began to trim the hair of this or that client beneath the sign still reading "Shoe Repair and Locksmith." But most of the time he stood in the doorway waiting for customers. Meanwhile the shop has closed again, beneath the sign still reading "Shoe Repair and Locksmith." When the first railroad line was to resume service, all the nation's children were called on to pull up the grass growing between the tracks along the entire stretch. They were given points for every meter of track they weeded, and the girl who collected the most points was featured in the newspaper along with her squint. On its maiden voyage along this cleanly weeded stretch of track, the garland-adorned train hit a bomb and was blown up along with the conductor, crew and guests of honor. Hereupon the reintroduction of train travel was postponed. That's what I read, anyhow, her father says. For the last few days he's been allowed to read the newspaper. Just imagine, he says.

The signature with which she confirmed that the house with all its furniture now belongs to her is a hybrid. The first name that her parents gave her at birth paired with her parents' last name. Her name is thus a meeting place for all sorts of different people, just like all the other words in the language or the money that passes through so many hands, some of which might some day have occasion to chop off others and put them in packages. House and furniture are intended to serve as compensation, she was told. For everything she'd been through. She sells only the piano. Her father's room still smells of tobacco, though it's been quite some time now since anyone has smoked there. He's even allowed to have tobacco now, her father says, it's just like a hotel. Just wait, he says, it won't be much longer now. No, she says, definitely not. Meanwhile she looks after the house and everything within it: the wardrobes, mirrors, highboys, chandeliers and gothic benches.

Outside, something or other is constantly being blown up these days: the arms, legs, bellies and heads of people waiting at bus stops or standing in line at some agency or simply out for a walk. Things can't go on like this much longer, her father says, you'll see, the country needs to be put back in order again.

The young man and the young woman now consist only of paper. From time to time they smile to themselves, always in the same way, in the one or the other newspaper. If a person has gone missing, the supply of pictures is quite naturally cut off at a certain point. The young woman who gave birth to her is already starting to look like her sister in these pictures, and the young man who fathered her appears to be her brother. Things might change, you never know. Some day the young woman who gave birth to her will look like her daughter, and the young man who fathered her like her son. She can use the newspaper to polish the window-panes, or fold it into a little square to stick beneath a wobbly table leg, she can also, when she's cleaning vegetables, lay out the newspaper underneath and afterward wrap the peels of the onions, carrots and potatoes in it and place the soft, round parcel in the trash.

When her father asks her on her visits, during which she is separated from him by a pane of glass, whether she doesn't want to visit her mother as well, she says: Uh-huh. Change is all very well and good, her father says. But eventually one needs to have a foundation to build on. Those who do the most criticizing, her father says, are the ones who don't want to work. It's easy to say what's wrong, her father says, if you aren't one of those who bear *the responsibility. It's always easier to break things down than to build something up. A body consists primarily of hydrocarbons, her father says, and decomposes with the help of worms and wood lice when placed quite normally beneath the earth, but one might also, provided one has the technical knowledge, transform it into a diamond. Into something that will last. And that's a great deal more interesting, isn't it, her father asks. Yes, she says, it is.*

Worms and wood lice.

After three years her mother comes home and goes back to frying fish, meat and vegetables in the kitchen in the evenings, washing lettuce, stirring and chopping, while she herself sits at the living room table drawing up contracts or talking on the telephone. In the newspapers in which her mother wraps up the peels after cleaning the vegetables, new, unknown faces are meanwhile smiling. Time marches on, her father says to her when she visits him in prison, as she does every Friday. Every Saturday morning she joins her mother in cleaning the house from top to bottom. Never again will a stranger cross my threshold, her mother declares. No, she replies. Whenever her mother suggests to her that she finally come along to see the woman who knows what to do with hands, feet and faces to keep them looking young, she would like to see her mother fall down the stairs or out the window, or stab herself accidentally while slicing bread. Two years later, her father comes home as well.

Translator's Afterword by Susan Bernofsky

ALL BOOKS ARE TRANSFORMED by their translations. Since in Jenny Erpenbeck's *The Book of Words* the transplantation from German to English obscures certain fundamental points about the story being told, I've decided to append a few comments to orient the reader. On its surface, the novel has nothing to do with Germany at all; it is set in a foreign country, apparently located in South America, that remains curiously undefined, as nameless as the little girl who is the book's protagonist. To be sure, a number of clues invite us to think of Argentina in particular as a model for this country: This is where Saint Difunta Correa is most commonly worshipped, and the novel's first two epigraphs come from an article on the victims of political purges during Argentina's "dirty war" (1976–1983). But the basic anonymity of Erpenbeck's setting is crucial: *The Book of Words* is no historical novel, it is a parable of life lived in a state of endless subtraction, with words, objects and people constantly being taken away. This is the most innocent possible perspective on life in a totalitarian society where freedoms are drastically limited, divergent opinions outlawed, and critics tortured and killed.

One of the many countries this parable might invite us to think of is the East Germany of Erpenbeck's childhood, where mysterious disappearances, interrogation and imprisonment were sometimes a part of life. Occasionally—such as when the girl's father uses the word "material" to refer to the corpses of torture victims—the book invokes the sort of bureaucratic language associated with the Stasi, the secret police of the German Democratic Republic, and the Socialist Unity Party that backed it. This co-opting of language to frightening political ends underlies the book's nostalgia for a time when the words just meant what they meant, when they were "stable, fixed in place" and "intact."

But the novel's "Germanness" comes out most clearly in all the German children's songs and nursery rhymes incorporated into it, some of them as unsettling as the tales of the Grimms. These include a traditional St. Martin's Day song; a rainy-day rhyme promising a sick child a swift return to health; a ditty about a little bird arriving with a letter from a child's mother; a ballad about washerwomen; lines from *The Magic Flute*; and a mealtime prayer. Also featured is a popular rhyme for bouncing a child on one's knee as if on horseback: *Hoppa, hoppa Reiter, / wenn er fällt, dann schreit er. / Fällt er in den Graben, / fressen ihn die Raben. / Fällt er in den Sumpf, / macht der Reiter plumps!* (Hippity-hop rider, if he falls he'll scream. If he falls in the ditch ravens will eat him. If he falls in the bog he'll go plop.) There are even a pair of magic spells that represent a deep stratum of German historical consciousness. The Second Merseburg Incantation quoted in the epigraph is a healing spell for broken bones (originally used on an injured horse); the manuscript dates from the ninth or tenth century, though the spell may be much older. The second spell quoted in the novel, its purpose to staunch a bleeding wound, is recorded in an eleventh-century manuscript. Not every song and rhyme quoted in the novel is German—the attentive reader may notice an aria from *Rigoletto* as well as a 1978 hit list sampler—but most are, and their cultural specificity sticks out in a setting otherwise marked as South American.

While these rhymes, songs and spells have been translated (or in a few cases replaced with equivalents sharing similar resonances), remembering that they represent a cultural heritage of Germanness is important for the background story of Erpenbeck's novel. We are told several times that the girl's mother, whom the girl hates and fears, is an outsider in their country: she has "eyes the color of water," which she attempts to hide in church by keeping them cast down, and was born somewhere far away, in a place where there is snow. We see our young narrator puzzling over an old photograph of her mother as a baby wrapped up in blankets and lying on a sled, her cheeks flushed with the cold. The girl has never met her maternal grandfather, but when near the end of the book her father begins to talk to her about torture techniques he has used, he also reveals a particularly grisly bit of family history: "Your mother's father, your grandfather, whom you never met, used to toss children into the air on the other side of the world if they were small and light enough, toss them into the air like birds and then shoot them before their parents' eyes." This "other side of the world," we are invited to imagine, is Germany under National Socialist rule—yet another state with a legacy of torture, and one from which many a torturer fled after the second world war, finding refuge in South America. These German songs may really be, quite literally, part of this little girl's childhood. *The Book of Words*, its eternally sunshine-filled present tense notwithstanding, takes us back to Nuremberg, the Black Forest, and a bunker in Berlin.